Buried Treasures
of the South

Buried Treasures
of the South

*Legends of Lost, Buried, and Forgotten Treasures—
from Tidewater Virginia and Coastal Carolina to
Cajun Louisiana*

W.C. Jameson

August House Publishers, Inc.
L I T T L E R O C K

Published by August House, Inc.,
P.O. Box 3223, Little Rock, Arkansas, 72203,
501-372-5450.

Printed in the United States of America

10 9 8 7 6 5 4 3 2 1

LIBRARY OF CONGRESS CATALOGING-IN-PUBLICATION DATA

Jameson, W. C., 1942–
Buried treasures of the South : legends of lost, buried, and forgotten treasures,
from Tidewater Virginia to coastal Carolina to Cajun Louisiana /
W. C. Jameson — 1st ed.
p.   cm.
Includes bibliographical references.
ISBN 0-87483-286-1 (acid-free paper) : $9.95
1.Treasure-trove—Southern States. I. Title.
G525.J355   1992
975—dc20   92-33308

First Edition, 1992

Executive: Liz Parkhurst
Project editor: Kathleen Harper
Design director: Ted Parkhurst
Cover design: Wendell E. Hall
Typography: Lettergraphics, Little Rock

This book is printed on archival-quality paper which meets the
guidelines for performance and durability of the Committee on
Production Guidelines for Book Longevity of the
Council on Library Resources.

AUGUST HOUSE, INC.   PUBLISHERS   LITTLE ROCK

This book is dedicated to my son
Will
who has been my traveling companion and top
hand on so many expeditions

Contents

Prologue

Ever since I was ten years old, I have been collecting tales and legends of lost mines and buried treasures throughout much of the Western Hemisphere. Why? Because I have always been fascinated by stories of incredible wealth lost and found, wealth that may lie mere inches below the ground or just a few feet inside some long-abandoned mine shaft.

I am also fascinated by those people who spent their lives searching for treasure. Many of them became wealthy overnight as a result of discovering gold or silver, and I am curious as to how this affected their lives. Some found treasure only to lose it and spend the rest of their lives searching for it again. Even today, men and women pursue the dream of finding a buried treasure or a lost mine. I want to know what motivates them, what has caused them, in some cases, to give up jobs, home, and even family to chase an elusive, perhaps only mythical, hoard or forgotten gold mine or hidden cache.

I, too, am a hunter of lost treasures. For years I have poured over maps both old and new, I have traveled from Canada to Mexico tracking down leads, and I have hiked and packed into some of the most wild and remote country in the nation. So strong is the lure of buried treasure that I have dedicated weeks at a time to its pursuit, and have endured rattlesnakes, cougars, bandits, hunger, and thirst along the way. On several occasions I have nearly lost my life in falls from steep cliffs and close encounters with poisonous snakes, and have been trapped in collapsed mines and caught without food or water in areas far from help.

Some of these adventures yielded treasure and some did not, but I have never been disappointed. Today I pursue lost mines, buried treasures, and their associated tales as actively as I did thirty years ago, and I foresee no lessening of this passion.

Most of my treasure hunting and story collecting has taken place west of the Mississippi River. For years I heard bits and pieces of treasure tales originating in the American South, but paid them little attention, believing that the most promising locations for lost fortunes lay in the Rocky Mountains of the West, the deserts of the Southwest, and the remote, forgotton valleys of the Ozarks. I discovered I was wrong.

I grew intrigued as each year I encountered more and more treasure tales coming from the South—a buried fortune on some plantation here, a lost Cherokee gold mine there, Civil War loot hidden long ago and now nearly forgotten. I gradually became captivated by the prospect of great tales of treasures in the South.

An extended journey to the Appalachian Mountains in 1990 to complete research for a book (*Buried Treasures of the Appalachians,* August House, 1991) brought me in contact with many Southerners and their tales of lost mines and buried treasures. I was enchanted by their stories and spellbound at the prospect of delving into them.

When I returned home, I got out my collection of Southern treasure tales, studied them, and felt a growing enthusiasm to research them, track them down, and collect others.

Within a few weeks I had made up my mind. After some preliminary research, I set out for the American South in search of the stories I believed existed there.

I drove the highways—the secondary and even the tertiary roads throughout Alabama, Georgia, Louisiana,

Mississippi, North Carolina, South Carolina, Tennessee, and Virginia. I spent countless hours in libraries and courthouses searching for the stories, searching for facts. I questioned experts at colleges and universities. I followed leads to people who had various connections to many of the lost treasures, and visited numerous sites associated with the stories, locations that no doubt held treasures or secrets to treasures hidden long ago.

Most important, I met and visited with the people of the South, many of whom related tales passed down in their unique and colorful oral tradition. From them I discovered more than I did from libraries or professors. Not only did I listen to their tales and versions of legends, I also learned of their attachment to the land and its residents, their passion for the South, and their sense of belonging to a special place which had produced and shaped them. Each place I visited in the South was, in fact, a treasure; each person I had the good fortune to meet, a jewel.

When I left the South, I came away with a new and vigorous appreciation of its landscape, its way of life, and something else—its incredible heritage of folklore, the tales, traditions, and beliefs handed down over generations. Quite unselfishly, Southerners shared their tales of lost mines and buried treasures, enhancing much of what I had already collected.

For many Southerners, the tales are not merely stories, they are real. These people firmly believe in the existence of the lost mines and hidden fortunes, and are convinced that they will someday be found—it is only a matter of time.

Introduction

The South! Throughout much of the United States, the unique geographic region we call the South evokes a myriad of stereotypes, some of which are accurate, some not.

Many people hearing the term "the South" conjure up images of vast plantations sporting multi-storied, multiple-columned homes with genteel, fashionably clad residents sitting on the wide front porches, sipping mint juleps. Others visualize remote swamps filled with dangerous reptiles and renegades, cloaked in heat and humidity. Still others recall images from the days of slavery, and the fact that the South was the principal setting for the bloody War Between the States.

To some extent all of the above evocations are true, but none necessarily sums up the heart and soul of the South. This broad geographic region can be described most accurately in terms of its diversity—diversity in both the physical environment and in the many cultures that have contributed to its current makeup. Lying between the Potomac River and the Gulf Coast, this area has a regional distinctiveness that cannot be denied and a colorful history that cannot be ignored. Its contributions to American culture and folklore are immeasurable.

THE PHYSICAL SETTING

The South consists of a broad array of physical landscapes and environments that appealed to a variety of people from the north and east who arrived in the area and settled portions of it. The environment itself subsequently spawned successive generations of people characterized by their individuality and determination to exist in a rugged and sometimes unforgiving land. To be a Southerner was not always easy, but to be a Southerner was to be proud.

The Appalachian Mountains are located in the northernmost portions of the American South. Folded, faulted, crumpled, uplifted, and highly eroded, they are replete with a variety of environments, wildlife, and natural resources. Their isolated hollows and high, naked ridges inhibited heavy human settlement until relatively recent times.

Though mostly unsuitable for agriculture save for some high meadows and rich, narrow bottomlands, the Appalachians occasionally yielded precious minerals in the form of gold and silver, which attracted numerous prospectors and miners long before the Civil War raged throughout the region.

Even today, many of the shadowy, remote areas that exist within this beautiful yet sometimes mysterious range yield a wealth of stories about fortunes in gold and silver mined from the rocky hills, some of it lost or abandoned, some of it reclaimed. Many of the residents living in these regions still believe in the existence of the long-lost mines and elusive caches of precious ore and stolen booty.

Extending from the rugged Appalachian Mountains to the Atlantic Ocean and the Gulf of Mexico is a vast, somewhat flat area geographers refer to as the coastal plain. This broad plain is generally topped with deep, fertile soil, and underlaid with layers of sedimentary rocks which dip gently away from the mountains and toward the sea. It was formed, in large part, from deposits of fine sediment during a period when sea levels were much higher.

Early settlers soon discovered that this plain, with its fertile soil and good drainage, would support many different crops. In time, great Southern plantations were established, where vast fields of cotton, corn, tobacco, and sugar cane flourished.

Fortunes were made and lost here. Many plantation owners, distrustful of banks and bankers, buried the proceeds of their harvest in secret locations on their farms, locations that were forgotton or lost with the passing years.

The plantations are no more, but agricultural pursuits continue on the coastal plain today, though they are considerably more diversified and mechanized than they were a hundred years ago.

The portions of the coastal plain adjacent to the sea generally tend to be flat, low, and swampy—grim prospects for agriculture unless the land has been drained. Estuaries located where the lowland merges with the sea are often populated with an impressive variety of wildlife.

Along these coastal margins, modern cities like Norfolk, Charleston, Savannah, Mobile, and New Orleans have evolved from historic seaports which were in use for many years. During the last few centuries these ports served as settings for the comings and goings of merchant ships, immigrant vessels, and galleons commanded by dreaded pirates, and became the favorite haunts of notorious buccaneers such as Blackbeard and Stede Bonnet. Many present-day residents of these areas maintain that the cutthroats of yesteryear buried portions of their great fortunes nearby.

THE CULTURES

Long before white settlers ever passed through the northern valleys into the South or arrived on its shores from other nations, the region was populated by numerous tribes of native Americans.

Though the Indian tribes of the South occasionally warred with one another, they were by and large more peaceful than their western counterparts and more interested in farming and maintaining stable, progressive villages than in taking scalps and counting coups.

Foremost among the Southern tribes was the Cherokee, both in sheer numbers and in the complexity and sophistication of their social structure. The Cherokee were also noted for their well-managed farms and fine livestock. Other Indians residing in the American South included the Creek, Choctaw, Chickasaw, and dozens of smaller tribes.

In addition to agricultural pursuits and some hunting, the Southern Indians also engaged in mining from time to time, extracting quantities of gold and silver from the rock of the Appalachian Mountains for use in fashioning jewelry and ceremonial ornaments.

The first white people these Indians encountered were the Spanish explorers. Under the leadership of Hernando de Soto, a large party of Spaniards composed of soldiers, miners, and Jesuits explored much of the South, assessing the land and its inhabitants as well as searching for wealth in the form of gold and silver with which to fill the Spanish treasury.

Though many encounters between the Indians and the Spanish explorers were friendly, more often than not confrontation and conflict resulted, especially when the Spaniards attempted to take the gold and silver belonging to the natives.

The Spanish reign in the South was relatively short-lived, but the region soon proved attractive to other whites. Many Anglos whose families had initially settled in the mid-Atlantic and New England regions of the United States were beginning to feel closed in and sought new lands to move into, new soil to till. Many migrated to the fertile plains and gold fields of the West, but a significant number traveled southward. Some found the narrow bottomlands of the Appalachians to their liking and established small

16

farms in isolated portions of the range. Others, encountering the more abundant fertile soils of the coastal plains, realized the possibilities for establishing larger and more productive farms there.

Much of the land perceived as desirable by the white newcomers was already occupied by Indians, and competition between the two cultures often resulted in casualties. As it became clear that the Indians were outnumbered, the newcomers began to put pressure on their government, which in turn ordered the removal of the native Americans to new and relatively unknown lands in Indian Territory, in what is present-day Oklahoma.

As time passed and agriculture thrived, it became apparent that large-scale growing and harvesting of crops such as cotton, corn, tobacco, and sugar could not be accomplished without a large supply of physical labor. Slaves were subsequently imported into the region to satisfy the economic goals of the early plantation operators, and blacks were introduced into the growing and changing culture of the South.

Eventually, the cultural and economic ideals of the Southerners began to clash with those of the residents of the North, and disagreements arose which eventually evolved into a bloody war between the two sections. The Civil War ripped the Southern economy and way of life to shreds, an event from which large portions of the South were slow to recover.

After the war, the region settled into a new order. Agriculture was still important but it was now accomplished on a sharecropper and tenant farmer basis. As more and different people moved into the area, industries were established, roads and railroads were constructed, local governments evolved, and the economy became more diversified. Cities grew, providing homes and opportunities for people of different races and ethnic backgrounds. The South was beginning to take on characteristics similar to those of the rest of the United States.

BURIED TREASURE IN THE SOUTH

Because the South is rich in cultural and environmental diversity, it is correspondingly rich in history and folklore. Southern history has long been a topic of study in college classrooms around the country and is increasingly coming under the scrutiny of scholars everywhere.

In addition to history, Southern folklore is experiencing a revival as scholars, historians, collectors, folklorists, and writers descend on the area in an attempt to discover, collect, and preserve various aspects of Southern myths, legends, and tales. As most people believe that there is usually an element of truth in every folktale, the study of such stories often provides insight into the history and culture of a particular region.

One specific genre of Southern folklore that is gaining recognition and growing in popularity is the lore of lost mines and buried treasures. Long before the Spanish explorers ever arrived in the South, the Indians in the region had been mining gold and silver from the rock matrix of the Appalachian Mountains, and many are the tales handed down in the oral tradition by native Americans concerning treasures accumulated, hidden, buried, lost, and sometimes found.

The Spanish also contributed heavily to the treasure tales of the South. Because part of their mission was to locate precious minerals, they became fascinated by the abundance of gold and silver possessed by some of the tribes they encountered and the evidence of ore they discovered in the mountainous regions. In some instances the Spaniards simply took the gold and silver from the Indians. In others they enslaved them and forced them to work in their own mines, extracting more ore for the European invaders. Spanish documents uncovered in monasteries in the Iberian Peninsula testify to the riches taken from the mines in the mountains of the American South and transported across the Atlantic to the Old World.

As increasing numbers of other white settlers arrived in the area, many of them also became aware of the presence of gold and silver. Some made friends with the Indians and obtained quantities of the ore in trade. Others, like the Spaniards before them, simply robbed the native Americans of their wealth. And still others discovered gold and silver for themselves and operated mines of their own. Their stories of wealth, lost mines, and buried treasure were told around campfires, in homes, and in taverns, and handed down through succeeding generations.

During the Civil War, the armies of both the North and the South needed money to support their respective causes. Towns were often sacked, farms raided, and money and valuables taken whenever the opportunity arose. Some of this wealth was used to purchase arms and ammunition and to pay the soldiers, but on many occasions it was hidden and either forgotten or lost.

The tales of lost mines and buried treasures are attractive to more than just those with an interest in folklore. Many people throughout the country have been lured by the promise of wealth lying buried in some remote location in the South, or the prospect of an abandoned mine in the Southern Appalachians that might conceal millions of dollars in gold or silver ingots. Treasure hunters, explorers, and adventurers still arrive in the South, on the trail of buried wealth they believe is lost or hidden there. Some search their entire lives for these riches and find nothing. Others are luckier and come away with fortunes.

Throughout the history of the South, many settlements and communities sprang up and died, many cultures were displaced or destroyed, and many individuals, unable to make a living, had to move on. But the South survived.

And like the South, the tales which are so much a part of the people and the land also endured. The stories of lost mines and buried treasures have the distinct flavor of the South, of Southern people and Southern places. They are all colorful narratives of a time not long past.

ALABAMA

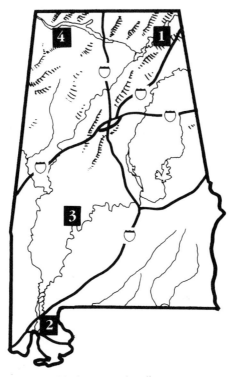

1. Yuchi Gold of Paint Rock Valley
2. The Lost Coin Caches of the Perdido River Ferryman
3. Abandoned Treasure in Cahaba
4. The Treasure of Red Bone Cave

Yuchi Gold of Paint Rock Valley

It was the last year of the seventeenth century, and the small company of Spanish soldiers was about to undertake a most perilous journey, a journey to transport millions of dollars' worth of gold bars across the frontier to a distant point on the east coast of Florida.

For six long years, the Spaniards had labored in a rich gold mine deep in the heart of the Sierra Madre of northern Mexico. The original company of some two hundred officers, soldiers, miners, and priests had been assigned by the Spanish government to extract the precious metal from the grudging rock of the mountains. The original force had been reduced to sixty by Indian attacks, disease, and starvation, but with the help of Indian slaves, they stayed and continued the mining operation.

At the end of each month, the raw gold was melted down and poured into molds to make brick-sized ingots which were stacked along one wall of the mine awaiting transport to Spain. Sometimes as many as several hundred gold bars would accumulate before an escort from the government leaders arrived.

About three times a year, a big pack train—about sixty mules—would come from Mexico City with supplies. Slaves would then load the bars onto the mules, and the wealth would be taken to the Mexican gulf coast, transferred to a ship, and sailed to the Iberian peninsula.

The officers in charge of the mine began to cast greedy eyes on the gold. After the first year of operation, they agreed among themselves to cache every fifth ingot in a secret hiding place, intending to ship the gold clandestinely to Europe and set themselves up in business. When enough gold had been stockpiled to satisfy the officers, they planned to pack it north, cross the Rio Grande, and make their way to a designated point somewhere on the northeast coast of Florida. Arrangements had been made with a renegade ship captain to haul the riches back to Europe, where the officers intended to live out their lives in splendor.

Sometime during the winter of 1699, the officers decided they had put aside enough gold to make them wealthy men. They were ready to undertake the journey to Florida. The gold was loaded onto pack mules, and the unsuspecting enlisted men were commanded to escort the vast wealth across the continent. Before abandoning the area, the Spaniards executed all the Indian slaves, stacked their bodies in the mine, and sealed and disguised the entrance.

Several days later, the party crossed the Rio Grande near what is now Del Rio, Texas, and proceeded eastward. There were many rivers to cross in the Texas country, and the spring rains had swollen most of them to flood stage, making travel difficult and often delaying the march for days at a time. The Spaniards also had to deal with hostile Indians along the way, and by the time they reached Louisiana, their numbers had decreased significantly. With fewer men, the pack train of some twenty mule-loads of gold ingots was becoming increasingly difficult to maintain.

As the Spaniards neared the Louisiana gulf coast, they learned the Indians in the area were preying on travelers and trappers. Visitors to the region were often tortured, killed, and mutilated. The heads of victims were put on pikes and set in the middle of the trail as a warning to outsiders.

Because of the Indian depredations, the Spaniards made a wide swing northeast and passed through what is now central Mississippi and Alabama. Here they were attacked several times by still other tribes, forcing them to veer even further northeast. Eventually they reached a point just north of present-day Tuscaloosa where the officers ordered a halt so that men and livestock might rest up from the arduous journey.

One evening while the Spaniards were dining around the campfire, a war party of some seventy Indians poured out of the forest and attacked and killed every one of them in minutes.

The Indians were of the Yuchi tribe, closely related to the Cherokee. Ordinarily, they were not warlike, but like most of the other tribes in the region, they resented the encroachment of outsiders on their land.

The Indians, who used gold to make jewelry, led the ingot-laden pack mules back to their village in Paint Rock Valley, about twenty miles east of present-day Huntsville. There, the Yuchi chief ordered the gold stashed in a nearby cave. He did not want any evidence of the intruders' wealth around should his village be visited by friends of the Spaniards.

Over the next several generations, Indians occasionally visited the cave to remove some of the gold for making jewelry, but other than the loss of those small amounts from time to time, the cache remained virtually undisturbed.

During the Indian removal of the early 1830s, the Yuchi tribe was ordered to vacate Paint Rock Valley. Before leaving, many of the Indians went to the cavern and divided some of the gold within. Several families tried to carry some of the heavy ingots on their journey along the Trail of Tears, but they were forced to bury them along the way.

Some members of the tribe escaped the military escort and fled eastward to Tennessee with their share of the gold, settling eventually at Henderson Ridge.

The greatest portion of the Spanish ingots remained in the cave.

Sometime in the mid–1920s, an aged Indian appeared at Paint Rock Valley leading two fine mules. He claimed he came from Henderson Ridge and was descended from the Yuchi Indians who had originally settled the valley. The old Indian was impressed with the farmlands which were once the site of the village of his forefathers, and he was friendly to all he met.

The Indian said he was looking for two able-bodied young men to help him load some heavy objects onto the mules, and soon acquired the services of two strapping youths, each about sixteen years old.

The old Indian, the boys, and the two mules left early the next morning and began a long trek out of the valley and into the limestone hills. From time to time, the Indian would call a brief halt while he checked notations on a very old map he carried. About an hour into the journey, the Indian told the youths they would have to be blindfolded the rest of the way. At first they demurred, but the old man said it was the Indian way of doing things, so they humored him and let their eyes be covered. With each of the boys holding onto the tail of a mule, the Indian led the way deeper into the hills.

The three had walked and climbed for another hour when the youths suddenly noticed the air had turned cooler and they could hear the echo of their own footsteps. The Indian removed their blindfolds, and they found themselves inside a great cavern with water dripping from ceiling and walls. The Indian lit a torch, handed each of the boys two burlap sacks, and led them deeper into the cave.

After another twenty minutes of negotiating several big boulders and narrow passageways, they came to a large chamber. Against one wall of the chamber were piled dozens of good-sized rocks, which the Indian asked the boys to remove. They did so and found an irregular jumble of hundreds of brick-sized bars of some kind of metal. One of the boys picked up a bar, hefted it, and suggested it might be lead because of the weight. The Indian merely nodded and asked them to fill the burlap sacks with as many of the bars as they could carry.

The three men made a total of four trips back into the chamber, carrying out burlap sacks containing three or four of the heavy ingots each time. With difficulty, the Indian loaded the bars into several stout leather packs which were tied to wooden pack frames on the two mules. When all the packs were full, the Indian had the boys cover the rest of the ingots with the large rocks they had removed earlier. Though they had carried out several dozen, hundreds still remained in the chamber deep within the cave.

When they were ready to leave, the Indian again blindfolded his two helpers. Assured they could not see anything, he led them back to the valley. The next day, the old Indian was seen leaving the area leading the two heavily laden mules toward Tennessee. It was the last time he was seen.

Several years later, the two boys—now grown men with families—heard the tale of the rich store of Spanish gold ingots cached in a limestone cavern somewhere back in the mountains surrounding Paint Rock Valley. It was then they realized they had carried gold, not lead, out of the cave for the old Indian.

For many years afterward, the two men tried to find the cave again, but they never did.

Lost Coin Caches of the Perdido River Ferryman

The Perdido River is a slow-moving stream that flows southward from southern Alabama to the Gulf of Mexico. For nearly fifty miles it serves as the boundary between the extreme western end of the Florida Panhandle and the bootheel of southwestern Alabama. For many years, the Perdido River presented an occasional obstacle to travelers going from Pensacola to Mobile. During periods of heavy rain the river would swell and become impassable. Westward travelers, along with their wagons and livestock, would often be forced to remain encamped on the eastern shore for weeks at a time, waiting for the waters to recede enough to allow crossing.

Recognizing the economic potential of a ferry crossing, a young man named Henry Allen Nuñez established one in 1815. As roads improved, stage lines evolved, and more citizens sought opportunities and free land in Oklahoma, Texas, and California, a significant westward migration began. As a result, the Nuñez ferry on the unpredictable Perdido River provided a much needed service for travelers and an impressive income for Nuñez. For many years it was the only crossing for several miles in either direction.

Travelers who used the ferry often paid in gold and silver coins, and as the years passed, Nuñez, known locally as a very frugal man, amassed a small fortune. His habit was to place the day's fare in gold and silver coins into an empty wine cask. After several months, when the wooden cask was nearly full, Nuñez would attach a cover and bury it in some location near his home, which was close to the ferry. A distrusting individual, Nuñez revealed the locations of only two of an estimated seven buried casks to his wife.

For forty-seven years, Nuñez faithfully manned the ferry in foul weather as well as fair, and became an incredibly wealthy man. He was quite elderly when the War Between the States broke out, but despite his age and poor health he continued to operate the ferry. Throughout much of the war, the crossing was visited often by both Union and Confederate troops. Nuñez, whose sympathies lay with the South, cheerfully aided both sides in crossing the river, though he was never paid by either for his services. He decided it was best to keep the soldiers happy and not jeopardize his business or his life.

Union forces soon occupied the region. During a routine scouting mission near the ferry crossing, a Union officer heard stories of Nuñez's fortune and the likelihood that it was buried near his home. Seeing an opportunity to grow wealthy at the expense of the old ferryman, the officer gathered four of his most faithful enlisted men and rode to the crossing.

On arriving at Nuñez's home, the cavalry officer called the old man out and demanded he turn over his fortune to aid the Union cause. Nuñez, nearly seventy years of age, told the officer he'd rather rot in hell than provide a single coin to the hated Yankees. Enraged, the officer ordered his men to seize Nuñez and carry him to the nearest tree.

With great difficulty, the soldiers hung the struggling Nuñez up by his thumbs and lashed him numerous times across his back and legs. Nuñez's wife, fearful that her husband would not survive the ordeal, led the soldiers to one of the buried casks. After stuffing the gold and silver coins into their saddlebags and pockets, the Union cavalrymen departed and rode to Mobile, where they squandered most of their newfound riches on liquor and women.

It took several days for old Nuñez to recover from the severe lashing and torture, and while he recuperated his wife operated the ferry.

Approximately two weeks later, the soldiers returned. They told the old man they believed there was more than one cask of buried coins—and they wanted the rest of them. For the second time the defiant old man refused the demands of the soldiers and ordered them off his property.

Once again, they strung the old ferryman up to a tree and beat him severely, and as before, Mrs. Nuñez, fearing her husband would be killed, showed the soldiers the location of a buried cache of coins.

After filling their saddlebags, the soldiers retraced their route to Mobile. A few days later, the Union company to which the cavalrymen were attached was assigned to Tennessee, and they were never seen at the crossing again.

Nuñez failed to recover from his second beating. Confined to his bed for several weeks, he eventually developed pneumonia and, too weak to resist the infection, died.

Unaware that as many a five more buried casks of gold and silver coins existed, Nuñez's wife quickly sold the ferry operation, the house, and the land, and went to live with relatives in Georgia.

Today it is difficult to pinpoint the original location of the old Perdido River ferry crossing, but historians have determined it is near the junction where U.S. Highway 90 crosses the river. All evidence of the Nuñez home has long since disappeared, but a systematic search of the area with sensitive metal detectors may yield one or more of the long-lost coin caches of the old ferryman.

Abandoned Treasure in Cahaba

Cahaba, Alabama, is historically unique and fascinating for several reasons. For one thing, it was the first state capital, having been established in 1819. The town also became a haven for a wealthy class of people who settled in the area—millionaires were plentiful and mansions could be found on most of the streets of this pleasant town on the west bank of the Alabama River.

The site at which Cahaba was located was subject to periodic severe flooding, and during the town's history three major floods struck the region and caused extensive damage. In 1865, as a result of unfortunate timing between a threatened raid by Union troops and a disastrous flood, millions of dollars in family fortunes, jewelry, and priceless household artifacts were buried and never recovered.

When Alabama joined the Union in 1819, it was of course necessary to choose a capital. After intense lobbying by Governor William Bibb, the town of Cahaba was selected. Located at the confluence of the Alabama and Cahaba Rivers just downstream from present-day Selma, Cahaba was described as a bountiful site with excellent fresh-water springs. Once selected, it grew rapidly and soon became one of the wealthiest towns in the state.

Attracted by the fertile valley and its clean environment, many of the state's wealthiest citizens moved to

Cahaba, and in a short time the area which was once the site of an Indian village and later a French fort boasted several schools, hotels, newspapers, and a bank.

The word *cahaba* is believed to be Choctaw for "high water." In 1825, as Cahaba was busily attaining the rank of a prominent and productive urban settlement, the aptness of the name was evidenced by the largest flood ever known to area residents. It swept through the town, virtually destroying everything in its path. Businesses and homes were washed away, very few structures were left standing, and the town had to be completely evacuated. Soon after the destruction of Cahaba, the state capital was moved to Tuscaloosa.

In 1828, the few remaining Cahaba residents resolved to rebuild their town. Initially, they made it an important steamboat stop on the Alabama River, and by 1830 it had regained some of the status it had held prior to the flood. Many of the wealthy who had abandoned Cahaba years earlier returned to rebuild their mansions and reestablish their businesses. Lured by the booming and industrious flavor of the town, still other millionaires moved to Cahaba.

But the boom was not to last. In 1833, just as it appeared that Cahaba was about to return to its former prominence, another flood completely destroyed the town. True to their persistent nature, however, the Cahaba residents again rebuilt, a bit more slowly this time, but nevertheless successfully. By 1850, this second reincarnation of the town of Cahaba had reached a population of 5,000 residents, and once again began to attract the wealthy and famous.

When the War Between the States broke out in 1861, a prison was built next to the town to house Union soldiers. The Cahaba Rifles, an infantry company of over 100 residents, fought with distinction at the battles of Antietam, Fredericksburg, and Vicksburg.

During the late spring of 1865, nearby Selma was attacked by Union troops. The town was looted and burned;

murder and rape were commonplace. Word quickly spread that the Union troops that had taken Selma were now on their way to Cahaba, eager to repeat their depredations.

In a panic, Cahaba residents quickly gathered their fortunes, their jewelry, and other valuables, and hastily hid them in secret locations throughout the town. Some were dropped into wells, many were lowered into the natural springs, some were buried in gardens, and others were hidden in yards. It is estimated that several million dollars' worth of gold and silver coins, jewelry, and silverware were hidden. Just as quickly, the Cahaba residents, utilizing whatever means of transportation they could find, abandoned the town.

The Union raid was never to materialize. Before the troops could arrive, another flood, this one a result of the recent heavy spring rains, came tearing down the valley, totally destroying the town for the third time in forty years. Once again buildings were leveled, trees were uprooted, and much of the environment around Cahaba was completely altered as a result of severe erosion in some places and heavy deposits of silt in others. By the time the flood waters receded several days later, little of the region bore any resemblance to the original site of Cahaba.

Weeks later, many of the residents returned to reclaim their valuables, but were unable to find the locations at which their fortunes were buried. Though some small portions of personal fortunes were recovered, most of the hidden treasure, millions of dollars' worth, was never found.

Undaunted, several of the more persevering residents attempted once again to rebuild Cahaba. During the early stages of this rebuilding process, however, a yellow fever epidemic swept through the area and killed hundreds. Cahaba was finally abandoned permanently in 1866.

Today, Cahaba, Alabama, is a ghost town. It does, however, get some small amount of tourism as a result of the fact that it has been designated an official point of interest. Portions of some of the rock buildings that survived the last flood are still standing, and the small town is replete with historic markers.

As far as researchers are concerned, an incredible fortune in coins, jewels, and other valuables lies buried in long-lost locations throughout the town, sites unknown to anyone now living.

The Treasure of Red Bone Cave

Somewhere on the north side of the Tennessee River near Muscle Shoals is an elusive limestone cavern which may contain several million dollars' worth of gold ingots and jewelry. This treasure cave has been known of for centuries, but efforts to locate it during the past 250 years have not succeeded.

Legend attributes the origin of the gold to Spanish explorers who came to this region under the leadership of Hernando de Soto. In 1538, Charles V of Spain gave de Soto ample funding and a company of more than six hundred men to travel to the New World to search for silver and gold. The ore was to be smelted, cast into ingots, and shipped to the motherland, Spain.

Arriving in Florida after months crossing the Atlantic Ocean, de Soto and his company of soldiers, miners, and priests traveled, explored, and prospected vast portions of the southern United States from the east coast to the Ozark Mountains. According to ancient records and documents found in Spanish monasteries, the explorers were successful, for they eventually shipped hundreds of millions of dollars' worth of gold and silver back to the Iberian peninsula.

As well as mining for it, de Soto's men took great quantities of gold from several of the Cherokee villages they encountered in their explorations. Though the Cherokee did not measure wealth in gold, they used the metal to fashion bracelets and other jewelry. When the Spanish saw the abundance of gold the Indians possessed, they took it by force, often killing hundreds of the red men in the process. The jewelry was melted down and formed into brick-sized ingots.

A Spanish detachment that had just raided several Cherokee villages was leading a gold-laden pack train of some forty horses when it chanced upon a friendly Chickasaw encampment in what is now northeastern Alabama. The settlement was a few miles south of the Tennessee River along a tributary that provided good water for drinking and crops.

As winter was coming, the Chickasaw invited the newcomers to remain in their village until the cold weather passed. The Spaniards accepted the invitation and lived for a time with the Indians, joining in their hunts for game.

When spring finally came, the Spaniards began preparing to travel to the southwest to rendezvous with de Soto at a location designated earlier. Before their departure, however, the leader of the party demanded of the Chickasaw chief some one hundred of the tribe's young women to accompany the soldiers on their journey. When the chief refused, the Spaniards became belligerent and threatening.

While they were loading their gold on the pack horses, the Spaniards were surprised by a sudden attack from the enraged Chickasaw. Panicked, the soldiers hastily mounted their horses and fled from the village, leaving behind the great treasure in gold ingots.

The Chickasaw pursued the Spaniards northward to the bank of the Tennessee River. With their retreat cut off, the soldiers turned and fought. The battle lasted nearly an hour, and when it was over, most of the Spaniards had been killed.

After returning to the village, the Chickasaw chief ordered all the treasure carried to a cave across the wide river to the north and concealed within it.

This done, the Indians ignored the great fortune in gold cached in the limestone cavern except when some small amount was needed to make jewelry and ornaments.

The Chickasaw village thrived during the ensuing years, and it was a large and happy community that greeted a young white trapper who entered the region in 1720 in search of beaver. The trapper wanted to try his luck along some of the small streams found in the area. He came to the Chickasaw village and requested permission from the chief to set his traps nearby.

The Chickasaw chief, impressed by the young man, granted permission and invited him to live in the village. He did so, and during the following weeks, the chief became very fond of the trapper.

The chief had only one child, a daughter, and as he was very old, he was concerned that she find a husband and provide him with a grandson who would eventually lead the tribe. The daughter had spurned the courtship of the many Chickasaw braves, and the chief was beginning to wonder if she would ever wed. The daughter did, however, find the young trapper to her liking, and soon the two of them were spending time together.

One night, about two months after he first entered the Chickasaw village, the trapper was awakened by two Indians. Without a word, they tied his hands behind his back and placed a blindfold over his eyes before he could identify them. He fought as hard as he could, but their combined strength was too much for him. Once he realized he was helpless, he ceased to struggle, and the Indians whispered that no harm would come to him if he followed their instruction.

All the rest of that night and the morning of the following day, the trapper was led through the woods.

Once while the group was stopped to rest, the blindfold slipped slightly from the captive's eyes, and he momentarily saw before him the wide expanse of the Tennessee River and the high limestone bluffs that rose in the distance beyond.

A few moments later, he was placed in a canoe and rowed across the river. After a brief hike, the three men came to a place where the air was cold and the ground was damp. The trapper could hear the squeaks of bats and realized he was inside a large cave.

Fifteen minutes further into the cave, the Indians called a halt, untied the trapper, and removed the blindfold.

The three men stood in a large chamber illuminated by torches. As the light flickered on the walls of the cave, the trapper looked around and recognized the chief of the Chickasaw village and one of his braves. The chief directed the trapper's eyes to one of the walls of the cave.

Stacked like cordwood against the far wall of the chamber were hundreds of ingots of pure gold, reaching nearly to the ceiling. At the foot of the stack were several chests filled with golden jewels and other valuables.

The chief told the trapper the tale of the long-ago Spaniards' visit. The chief also told him that the gold he saw in this room was only a part of the total amount hidden in the cave.

Taking the trapper to another chamber in the cave, the chief pointed to several skeletons propped against one wall. He said they were the bones of the warriors that had died in the battle with the fleeing Spaniards. The bodies were placed in the cave so their spirits could guard it against intruders.

The chief came forward and laid a hand on the trapper's shoulder. He told the young man that if he married his daughter, all the treasure in the other room would be his to keep. If he chose not to marry the daughter, he would be allowed to leave the village unharmed but was not to know the location of the treasure cave.

The trapper considered his options. If he married the chief's daughter and remained in the remote Indian village, the wealth would do him little good, as he would have no opportunity to spend it. Remembering his view of the river and the limestone bluff when the blindfold slipped from his eyes earlier that day, he believed he would be able to return and locate the cave on his own.

The trapper told the Chickasaw chief he wanted a few days alone to consider the offer. The chief agreed, reattached the bindings and the blindfold, and led the trapper from the cave.

Darkness fell long before the party could reach the village, and as they were all tired, the chief decided to camp for the night near the bank of the river. Late that night, the trapper killed the two Indians while they slept and threw their bodies into the river. He then fled on foot to Fort Rosalie in the Natchez Territory, reaching it after a harrowing journey of several days.

At the fort, the trapper invited an old friend to join him in his search for the great treasure of what he called Red Bone Cave, naming it after the skeletons of the red men he saw within it.

Hiding by day and searching by night, the two men spent the next several weeks trying to find the cave. The trapper's friend grew weary of the fruitless search and soon returned to Fort Rosalie.

Now alone, the trapper decided to return to the Chickasaw village. Wary at first, he was surprised when he was warmly welcomed by the Indians. He learned later that no one had ever known that the chief and his accomplice had kidnapped him and taken him from the village that night a few months earlier. The disappearance of the chief and the brave remained a mystery to the Indians.

Using the excuse of trapping for furs, the young man continued his search for Red Bone Cave. He eventually married the daughter of the dead chief and settled in the village, and though he searched for many years, he was never able to find the cave again.

In 1723, the trapper's wife died from malaria, and he eventually returned to Fort Rosalie. The settlement, however, had long since been abandoned. It lay in ruins, its people massacred years earlier by the Natchez Indians.

The trapper took up residence in the abandoned fort and remained there for the rest of his life. He made several more forays into the Chickasaw wilderness to find Red Bone Cave, but never succeeded.

In his later years, the old trapper often visited with the boatmen who plied the Tennessee River. He told them his strange tale of gold bars stacked like cordwood against the back wall of the elusive cavern.

Many thought the old trapper was crazy, but his tale has endured to the present and has inspired hundreds to search for the gold lying deep within Red Bone Cave.

GEORGIA

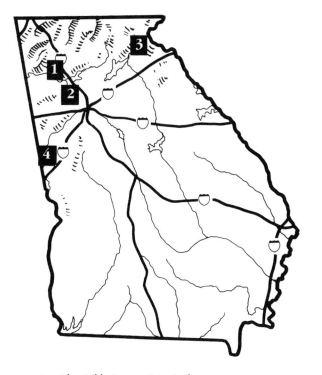

1. The Cobb County Coin Cache
2. The Peach Orchard Cache
3. Cave of Gold Nuggets
4. Mysterious Map Clue to $100,000
     in Gold and Silver Coins

The Cobb County
Coin Cache

During the early part of 1864, the War Between the States was gaining incredible momentum as thousands from the North and South alike were swept up in its fire and fury. When the Union forces began to make significant inroads into the South, many residents grew fearful for their lives and fortunes. Most Southerners were distrustful of banks and refused to consign their family fortunes to those establishments, which were in very real jeopardy as the Yankees raided town after town, robbing citizens and ransacking businesses and institutions in order to fill the treasuries of the Union army as well as their own pockets.

Many Southern residents traditionally buried their wealth on their own property, but Union soldiers learned of this practice early in the war, and often excavated large portions of the grounds around many stately Southern mansions in search of buried gold and silver coins and jewelry.

Aware of the Yankees' lust for their wealth, many Southerners retrieved their hidden fortunes, removed them from their property, and reburied them elsewhere, usually in some obscure location where the Union soldiers would not be likely to search. It is believed that millions of dollars' worth of Southern wealth were hidden in this manner. Most of it has not been recovered to this day.

One such case involved an unidentified Atlanta businessman who, fearful that the city would soon be under seige, packed more than 100,000 dollars in gold coins into several stout leather pouches. With the help of two slaves, the businessman loaded his fortune onto a departing Atlanta and Western Railroad passenger train at the downtown Atlanta terminal. Prior to boarding, the businessman had made arrangements for his cargo, his slaves, and himself to be dropped off at a somewhat remote location just across the Chattahoochee River in Cobb County, about fifteen miles northwest of the train station.

After crossing the Chattahoochee River, the train stopped and the three men laboriously unloaded the heavy pouches, depositing them next to the tracks. Once this was done, the train proceeded on to its destination.

The man divided the pouches among them, then led the two slaves about three hundred yards due northeast into the woods. At this point he made a blaze on a tree, and then proceeded approximately one hundred yards due north. Here the businessman carved a deep "M" and an "X" into a large oak tree which was located in a low area near a fresh-water spring not far from the Chattahoochee River.

Just a few paces from this tree, he ordered his slaves to deposit the gold-filled pouches into a shallow hole. (The hole was the result of the recent removal of an old rotted tree stump, presumably accomplished by the businessman a few days earlier.) Once the pouches were placed in the hole, they were covered with dirt, branches, and leaves, and the site was made to look exactly like the surrounding forest floor.

The businessman then seated himself against the bole of the tree he had just marked and drew a map showing the locations of the railroad track, the river, the marked trees, and the cache. Finally, he and the two slaves began the long trek back to Atlanta.

It was never known what became of the slaves, for within two days they disappeared. It was common belief at the time that they were killed by their owner because they knew the location of his buried wealth.

The businessman intended to return to his cache and retrieve his fortune in gold coins when the war died down, but fate was to thwart his plans. Apparently, the exertion of burying the coins and walking back to Atlanta was too much of a strain on his frail physical constitution, for within a few days he suffered a heart attack and died. His widow, in looking for the family fortune following the funeral, discovered the crude map showing the location of the buried cache. Family and business matters consumed her time for several months, but when her affairs were finally in order she began to make preparations to travel to Cobb County and retrieve the coins. Just as she was about to leave, General Sherman marched into Atlanta and burned it to the ground. The widow did not think it prudent to go after the fortune until hostilities subsided.

Finally the war came to an end, and the widow renewed her plans to locate the buried treasure. For several weeks she attempted to follow the directions to the cache, but she had a poor sense of distance and direction, and often became lost in the dense forest adjacent to the railroad tracks. Distrustful of others, she refused to let anyone accompany her on these searches. Eventually, frustrated with her inability to find the treasure, she abandoned her quest altogether and moved to Texas to live with relatives.

During the period when the widow was conducting her search, she spoke often with the conductor of the Atlanta and Western Railroad in order to pinpoint the precise location at which her husband had gotten off the train. On numerous occasions, the conductor was able to view the map which she carried, and each time he would commit as much of it as possible to memory, to be reproduced later. Finally, he constructed what he believed to be a reliable duplicate for his own use.

44

After the widow moved to Texas, the conductor took up the search. The time he spent looking for the buried treasure was interrupted all too often by the demands of his job, so he eventually quit in order to devote his energy to the pursuit of the Cobb County coin cache.

But the conductor had no better luck than the widow. It is likely that he inaccurately transcribed one or more of the landmarks when he attempted to duplicate the map, for after nearly a hundred fruitless trips into the woods between the railroad tracks and the Chattahoochee River, he finally gave up.

One day the old conductor related the tale of the buried coins to a young friend named John Maynard. Maynard was an engineer with the Atlanta and Western Railroad, and had known the conductor for several months prior to the old man's retirement.

Excited by the tale of the 100,000 dollar coin cache near the tracks, Maynard decided he would devote every spare moment of his life to searching for the treasure. At the first opportunity, he traveled by rail to Texas, where he met with the businessman's then aged widow. He convinced her to give him the original map drawn by her husband and he promised that, should he locate the buried treasure, he would divide it evenly with her. She eagerly consented to the agreement and gave him the map. Maynard returned to Atlanta, resigned his position with the railroad, and like the old conductor before him, spent the rest of his life searching for the treasure. He never found it.

In his old age, Maynard told of his search for the buried coins to a young friend named H.L. Denman. Denman was a fireman on the Nashville, Chattanooga, and St. Louis Railroad, and had known Maynard for several years. Initially, Denman was not in the least bit interested in the tale of treasure, convinced that it was nothing more than colorful local folklore. In 1907, Maynard showed Denman the original map and told him the details of his many attempts to locate the coin cache, but the fireman remained skeptical.

During the next several weeks, however, Denman mentioned the subject of the buried treasure to numerous other railroad men, and after listening to their versions of the story, became convinced that the treasure was, in fact, a reality. On a return trip to Atlanta, Denman was determined to obtain the map from Maynard and undertake a search himself. After arriving, however, Denman learned that Maynard had passed away a few days earlier, and that his survivors had accidentally burned the map along with a trunk full of worthless papers. Denman, like his predecessor, conducted several searches in the woods, near a point indicated to him earlier by Maynard. But because Denman had neither a map nor directions of any kind, his searches for the treasure were doomed to failure from the start.

The story of the buried 100,000 dollar treasure in Cobb County has entered the regional folklore of Atlanta and northern Georgia. Many are aware of the tale, and over the years hundreds have searched for the buried coins, but they have never been found.

In 1970, a man who has researched the tale for years located the tree with the "M" and the "X" blazed on the trunk. The markings, more than a hundred years old, were barely discernible and were noticed only as a consequence of their being highlighted by the setting sun.

According to the man, the area around the tree had changed considerably since the burial of the coins: there was no evidence of the spring, which had apparently dried up; thick underbrush had grown up throughout the region, making passage difficult in many places; and erosion had greatly altered the landscape.

Though he has returned many times to the blazed tree, the man has been unable to locate the cache of gold coins. He has shared his information with a young treasure hunter whom he befriended, and at this writing the two are planning another search, this time using sophisticated electronic detectors.

With luck and perseverence, the long-lost gold coin cache of Cobb County may eventually be found.

The Peach Orchard Cache

Businessman Duncan was a city man with city ways. He sported city clothes and liked to walk the city streets, passing the time of day with his city friends. His suits and vests were of the finest cloth, fashioned by the tailors he visited when he traveled north to Atlanta. His shoes were always as polished as his manner, for Duncan was of the wealthy class in Griffin, a town with a population of several thousand around the turn of the century, located some thirty-five miles south of Atlanta.

A prosperous businessman, Duncan was frugal in his other spending habits, and quite logical and prudent when it came to handling money. His several enterprises in Griffin, including a tavern and billiard hall, provided him with a steady and impressive income. Duncan lived the good life in a fine house backed by several acres of land on New Orleans Street. His family was comfortably provided for, and he was well thought of by his neighbors and considered by many to be one of the town's leaders.

Duncan did not place his money in a bank. In fact, like many residents of the South during this period, Duncan distrusted banks and preferred to keep his money stashed at home. Much to his wife's annoyance, Duncan left sacks and boxes of coins and bills in various locations throughout the house—in closets, in the tool shed, under the bed, and even in the kitchen cabinets.

Another thorn in Mrs. Duncan's side was the fact that her husband had a kind and gentle streak which occasionally caused him to bring home unfortunate travelers who were down on their luck and out of money. Duncan would provide the vagabonds with a hot meal and a bed for the night before sending them on their way. Mrs. Duncan worried that some of the men her husband brought to the house might be of a criminal mentality, and she often expressed the fear that they would discover the family fortune, slay them, and make off with the wealth. Many times she pleaded with her husband to gather up all of the money and deposit it in the bank, but Duncan always put her off, promising to take care of it at a later date.

Finally, after enduring several weeks of nagging on the subject, Duncan agreed to consolidate all of the sacks of coins and bills, and to transfer them to the bank for safekeeping. That evening, Duncan fetched an empty burlap coffee sack from the kitchen and went about the house placing the smaller sacks and containers of money into it. The sack normally held one hundred pounds of coffee beans, and by the time Duncan had gathered up all of his wealth, it was full. He tied it tightly at the top and promised his wife he would deliver the money to the bank the next day.

When morning arrived, Duncan bid his family good day, hoisted the sack across one shoulder, walked out the door, and headed down the street toward the bank. After two blocks, however, he cut across a field and made his way to the large peach orchard he maintained behind his house. In spite of what he had told his wife, Duncan had no intentions of placing what amounted to at least 100,000 dollars in a bank in which he had no confidence. Selecting a spot next to one of the nearly seventy-five peach trees, he excavated a shallow hole and buried his fortune.

That evening when Duncan returned home, nothing more was said about the money. The next day, Mrs. Duncan had occasion to go into the peach orchard, where she noticed some freshly turned dirt near one of the trees. Later that evening, she mentioned this to her husband, and in the same breath suggested it was probably the result of some animal rooting around. She seemed satisfied, and Duncan, concealing a slight grin, said nothing.

Several months later, Duncan, who was in his fifties and severely overweight, suffered a massive heart attack and was confined to bed for several days. Speaking was now very difficult for him, but on several occasions as his wife and daughter sat by his bedside, he would raise his hand slightly and point toward the peach orchard. He struggled very hard to explain something but was unable to utter any coherent sounds. Two weeks later he died.

Following the funeral, Mrs. Duncan made a trip to the bank for an assessment of the family fortune, and was stunned to learn that her husband had never made the promised deposit. For days she agonized over what might have become of the money—and then she recalled her husband's feeble attempts to communicate something about the peach orchard. Remembering the freshly turned earth she had seen in the orchard several months earlier, she deduced that Duncan had been trying to tell her that the money lay buried there.

Heartened at the prospect of retrieving the wealth, Mrs. Duncan ran to the peach orchard to search for the particular tree near which she believed it to be buried. But because so much time had passed, the ground around all of the trees looked exactly alike, and she had difficulty remembering exactly where she had seen the turned earth.

Taking a shovel from the tool shed, she dug several holes around a half dozen of the trees but found nothing. For several weeks thereafter, Mrs. Duncan, sometimes aided by her daughter, would spend entire days digging among the peach trees, sometimes reexcavating holes she had dug earlier. Frustrated and tired from the unsuccessful digging, Duncan's widow eventually hired a black man to make some excavations for her, but the treasure was never found.

When Duncan's daughter grew and married, she attempted to continue the search for the family fortune, but met with failure each time.

Someplace near old New Orleans Street in the city of Griffin, Georgia, located far behind the old house of businessman Duncan, lies buried a 100-pound sack of coins and turn-of-the-century bills. The peach orchard has long since vanished, but several residents claim to know exactly where it was once located.

On that spot, just a few inches below the surface, lies an incredible fortune.

Cave of Gold Nuggets

For nearly a dozen years before he died, Marvin Chambers knew of the existence of a fortune in gold nuggets lying on the floor of a cave located just a few minutes outside of the town of Toccoa, Georgia. Chambers had actually seen the nuggets—there were about twenty leather ore sacks filled with them—and he had carried back two large handfuls of the gold in his pockets. But though he had been in the cave and touched the gold, Chambers was completely ignorant of its location and spent the remaining years of his life trying to find the sight.

Marvin Chambers drove the Greyhound bus on a regular run from Charlotte, North Carolina, to Atlanta and back for seven years. He lived in Toccoa, and during his regular stop in that town he would visit and sip coffee with friends in the depot.

During one such stop, a friend of Chambers's pointed out a tall Cherokee Indian about fifty years of age who was eating lunch in a booth in the far corner. The friend told the bus driver that the Indian came to town on foot from somewhere in the nearby mountains about once every three or four weeks to purchase supplies. After filling his knapsack with coffee, sugar, flour, and a few other essential items, he hiked back into the mountains where he apparently lived. Chambers was only mildly interested in this story until his friend mentioned that the Indian paid for all of his purchases with gold nuggets.

Intrigued, Chambers watched as the Cherokee finished his lunch and left the bus station. The Indian was carrying a heavy knapsack and Chambers wondered if it contained gold.

About a week later as he was driving his bus into Toccoa, Chambers spotted the Cherokee walking along the highway toward town. On impulse, the driver pulled over, opened the door, and asked the Indian if he would like a ride into the station. For a moment the Indian looked questioningly at Chambers and the bus, but he finally climbed aboard and took a seat behind the driver. For the next couple of miles the two engaged in small talk. At the station, the Indian politely thanked Chambers, shouldered his knapsack, climbed out of the bus, and walked toward the center of town.

On several other occasions, Chambers gave the Cherokee a lift into Toccoa, and the two men soon became friends. One afternoon, after all the other passengers had gotten off the bus, the Indian told Chambers he wanted to show him something. Placing his knapsack in the middle of the aisle between the two front seats, he opened it up and pulled out a handful of gleaming gold nuggets. Chambers sucked in his breath in amazement at the quanitity and purity of the ore.

When he asked his friend where the gold came from, the Indian placed a finger to his lips and told the bus driver it was a secret, then lapsed into a tale. According to Indian legend, armor-clad invaders from Spain had entered the Cherokee homelands, discovered gold, and enslaved many members of the tribe to work in the mines. This continued for more than two years until the Indians finally revolted against their cruel masters. The subsequent uprising resulted in the liberation of the slaves and the death of every one of the Spaniards.

Because the Cherokee Indians perceived the shiny metal to be a source of evil, they gathered up all of the ore that had been stored in stout leather sacks by the Spaniards and hid it in a remote cave some distance from the village. Only a few members of the tribe knew the location.

Years passed, and white men began to move into this part of the South in great numbers. When it became clear to the Cherokee that the white men prized the shiny metal above all else, and when they realized that with it they could purchase weapons, ammunition, and food, the tribe's elders began making occasional trips to the cave for a bit of the ore.

More and more white settlers who coveted the prime Cherokee farmland came to the area and the Indians were eventually forced out and moved far to the west to live in Oklahoma Territory. The Indian told Chambers that he was born on a reservation in Oklahoma where he had often heard the tale of the huge cache of gold nuggets from an old tribal leader. About ten years ago, he explained, he decided to travel to Georgia to search for the gold which, if found, would be used for the good of the Indians. For several months the Cherokee lived in the mountains outside of Toccoa while he searched for the cave. He finally found it, and in the middle of the floor of a large room in the cavern he discovered about two dozen old leather sacks, tightly packed with rich gold nuggets, lying exactly where his ancestors had left them well over a hundred years earlier.

The Indian became convinced that it was his destiny to guard the gold and to use it only for good. Aside from taking small amounts of it from time to time to purchase food and supplies, he systematically and anonymously released some of it to certain Indian welfare agencies in the area.

The two men continued to visit with one another over the next few months, and one day the Cherokee told Chambers that he believed he was a good friend and an honorable man. If he wished to see the gold cache, the Cherokee told him, he would consider showing him the cave. He cautioned the bus driver, however, that he was never to try to return to the secret location or take any of the gold. Excited at the prospect of being close to such great wealth, Chambers could scarcely contain himself.

One afternoon two weeks later, as the Greyhound bus approached the Toccoa city limits, Chambers spotted his Cherokee friend waving at him from the side of the road. The driver stopped and invited the Indian aboard. Minutes later they arrived at the station and the passengers climbed out and filed into the lunchroom. The Cherokee asked Chambers to remain on the bus a moment longer to make arrangements to visit the cave. Chambers told his Indian friend he had a day off later in the week, and the Cherokee agreed to meet him then in front of the bus station.

On the appointed day, the Cherokee drove up to the station in an old, rusted-out 1937 Buick sedan and waved Chambers into the car. They drove around behind the station where it was explained to Chambers he would have to be blindfolded during the trip to the secret cave. Chambers readily agreed, and within minutes the Buick was back on the road.

Though blindfolded, Chambers was aware that the Indian drove through the town of Toccoa, circling city blocks several times. He presumed it was done to confuse him. Finally, the sedan picked up speed as it traveled down a straight stretch of highway and, as the sounds and smells of Toccoa gave way to the aromas and hums of the countryside, Chambers realized they had quit the town, though in which direction they traveled he was uncertain.

When the car stopped, Chambers estimated that the drive had taken about an hour.

He was helped out of the car and led on a steep climb up a hillside. Though the Cherokee did his best to assist him, the bus driver tripped and fell down several times, tearing his slacks and bloodying his knees. After about twenty minutes of rigorous climbing, the out-of-breath and weary-legged Chambers found himself entering a cooler enviornment on relatively flat ground. From the way the footsteps of the two men echoed, the bus driver realized they had entered a cave.

Chambers felt the blindfold being lifted from his eyes to reveal an open, high-ceilinged cavern. The only light was that from the torches carried by the Indian. A moment later, Chambers was guided to the center of the large room where he saw on the rocky floor before him numerous old leather bags stacked in a pile that came to his knees. Some of the bags had been opened, emptied, and tossed nearby, but there were at least twenty full ones remaining in the pile.

The Cherokee opened one and poured into Chambers's outstretched hands a quantity of almost pure gold nuggets. When the bag was half empty and Chambers's hands were full, the Indian told the bus driver to put the gold in his pocket and take it with him. It was a gift, he explained, for the friendship they had shared over the past few months. Chambers did so and then allowed himself to be blindfolded, led back down the steep hill, and helped into the Buick. The trip back to Toccoa took considerably less time than the trip out to the cave: the two men were back at the bus station in ten minutes!

After saying goodbye to the Indian, the greedy bus driver began to make plans to return to the cave and retrieve all of the gold. His only problem was that he had no idea where it was located, for hills and mountains surround Toccoa on all sides.

On his days off, Chambers would drive out into the countryside in an attempt to locate a steep hillside adjacent to the road. He found dozens of promising locations, but after spending hours climbing about the area, he always came away disappointed.

Chambers became so obsessed with finding the cache of gold nuggets in the lost cave that he eventually resigned from his job as a bus driver and devoted the rest of his life to the search. For seven years after initially laying eyes on the gold nuggets in the cave, Marvin Chambers spent nearly every day trying to relocate the site.

Once when driving down the highway, Chambers spotted the old Indian and pulled over. He told the Indian he had been searching for the cave and begged him to reveal its location. The Cherokee regarded the former bus driver for several minutes and finally told him he had betrayed a trust and was not worthy of sharing the gold. He told Chambers that, should he ever be caught in the treasure cave, he would be killed.

This threat had no effect on Chambers whatsoever, and he continued his search until he passed away in the 1950s. Several months after Chambers died, the Cherokee who had befriended him was killed as he walked along the highway into Toccoa. Ironically, he was struck by a Greyhound bus.

The gold, apparently well over a million dollars' worth, still lies on the floor of a lost cave in the mountains just beyond the city limits of Toccoa.

Mysterious Map Clue to $100,000 in Gold and Silver Coins

During the 1840s and 1850s, cotton plantations were springing up throughout the fertile farmlands of the South and the demand for labor was high.

A prosperous Georgia farmer named Lipscomb operated a large plantation near La Grange, a growing settlement located in the western part of the state near the Alabama border. Always the enterprising businessman, Lipscomb believed he could make a great deal of money supplying slaves to the plantation owners.

Both his plantation and his newly established slave trade flourished, and in a few short years he amassed approximately 100,000 dollars in profits, a huge fortune for that time.

Banks were scarce in the developing South, and the few that existed suffered from far too many inconsistencies in accounting and were highly susceptible to robbery. Lipscomb, like many other prosperous businessmen of the day, distrusted banks and preferred to hide his money on his own property. With the help of his most trusted slave, an elderly white-haired black man named Sledge, Lipscomb cached a total of about 100,000 dollars in gold and silver coins in two separate locations on the land near his house.

From time to time, Lipscomb would add to his hoard. Late at night when his family was asleep, he would quietly leave the house and tiptoe to the slave quarters, where he would awaken Sledge and order him to dig into one of the caches, where his most recent profits would be deposited. Lipscomb's wife and children were aware that the entrepreneur possessed a great deal of money, but they had no idea where it was hidden.

When the War Between the States broke out, Lipscomb feared he would be unable to continue with his slave trade should the North be victorious. As the war progressed, it became clear to him that the South was doomed to defeat. These concerns, along with his advanced age and deteriorating health, plunged Lipscomb into a spiral of depression and despair from which he never emerged. He began to neglect his family and farm; his only interest appeared to be his fortune.

From time to time, with the help of Sledge, Lipscomb would dig up his money, and for hours the plantation owner would sit on the ground and count the gold and silver coins over and over. It was the only thing that seemed to bring him any pleasure.

One evening Lipscomb decided to count his coins but was unable to locate Sledge. He became frantic when he realized that without the help of the black man he was unable to find the two caches. All night long the harried Lipscomb dug holes in his yard trying, to no avail, to locate the treasure. The next morning found him lying in the yard, exhausted and delirious.

Later that day when Lipscomb regained his lucidity, he concocted a plan that would assure him of being able to find his fortune anytime he wished. He decided to record the locations of the buried coins and then hide the directions in a place known only to him.

With the help of his trusted slave, Lipscomb located the two caches and placed a small stake in the ground above each one. Taking a heavy, ornamental lead plate from his wife's buffet, he carried it to a point in the front yard between the house and the well. From where he stood, Lipscomb could easily see the two stakes.

Next he took a gold coin from his pocket and hammered it into the center of one side of the plate. He etched in the soft lead an arrow pointing in the direction of the first cache, along with the number of paces between where he was standing and the site. Turning the plate over, he then hammered a silver coin into the opposite side and recorded the number of steps and a directional arrow pointing to the second treasure. After digging up a section of the turf at his feet, Lipscomb buried the plate so that each arrow pointed precisely in the direction of the respective treasure troves. The plantation owner would never again have to worry about finding his treasure.

Weeks passed, and Lipscomb grew more and more paranoid about the possibility of invading Yankees. He imagined Union soldiers numbering in the thousands were riding toward La Grange with the intention of taking his money from him. He even began to suspect Sledge of being in league with the thieving Union army and conspiring to dig up his treasure and spirit it away. In a fit of insane rage, he grabbed a gun and killed the unfortunate black man with one shot to the head.

Lipscomb's wife was alternately concerned for and in fear of her husband. On several occasions he accused her of trying to steal his fortune and threatened to kill her. His children were frightened of him and fled at his approach. Soon, the disturbed plantation owner was unable to sleep at night, preferring to sit up in his favorite chair, cradling a gun in his lap and babbling about his treasure.

Early one morning, Lipscomb's wife crept cautiously down the stairs to check on her husband. An ominous quiet reigned throughout the house, and he was nowhere to be seen. She was about to begin a thorough search of all of the rooms when she heard a piercing scream coming from the front yard. Looking out a second-story window, she saw her housekeeper cowering in fright near the well and pointing to something on the front porch. Hurrying outside, Mrs. Lipscomb found her husband's body hanging from a porch rafter. The unfortunate miser had committed suicide.

With the deaths of Sledge and Lipscomb, there was no one left alive who knew the location of the buried caches of gold and silver coins, and Lipscomb had told no one of the lead plate which he buried near the well in the front yard.

Mrs. Lipscomb was aware that her late husband had hidden a fortune but she, like everyone else, was ignorant of the location. With the help of several slaves, Mrs. Lipscomb supervised the excavation of numerous holes in the yard near the house, but no coins were found.

As the Civil War raged on it became clear to Mrs. Lipscomb that she would soon lose the farm and property, so she and her children fled to Texas to live with relatives. The plantation was abruptly abandoned, and neither Mrs. Lipscomb nor her children were ever heard from again.

Nearly one hundred years after the end of the Civil War, a resident of the nearby town of Franklin named Titus Johnson was exploring the ruins of the old Lipscomb plantation. As he stood near the long-abandoned well, he caught a glimpse of an object protruding from the ground several paces away. It appeared to be the edge of a platter. Curious, Johnson dug it up and beheld a strange artifact. It was a lead plate, but on one side a gold coin had been hammered into the center, and on the opposite side a silver coin had likewise been embedded. Completely unaware of the significance of his discovery, Johnson carried the plate home with him and placed it on a shelf in his garage.

A week later, Johnson retrieved the plate with the intention of removing the old coins and trying to find out if they were worth anything. As he pried one of them from the plate, he noticed some numbers and arrows had been scratched into the surface. Taking a brush, he cleaned the dirt from the plate and found Lipscomb's directions to his buried treasure. After cleaning the opposite side, he discovered more of the same.

Excited by his find, Johnson carried the plate back to the Lipscomb plantation and stood at the site at which he had unearthed it. After replacing the plate in the shallow hole, it became clear to Johnson that the directions inscribed on the two surfaces were useful only when the plate was lying on the ground in the precise position and alignment originally determined by Lipscomb. Unless the plate was oriented exactly as he found it, the directions were useless. Because he could not remember the exact position of the plate, Johnson was never able to locate the treasure.

Today, even the location of Lipscomb's old well is unknown. Johnson eventually returned the lead plate to the shelf in his garage, and when he passed away in 1981 his belongings were distributed among his relatives. No one knows what became of the plate bearing the directions to the treasure.

The front yard of the old Lipscomb plantation has been searched many times over the years and portions of it have been excavated, but the two caches of gold and silver coins, worth a tidy fortune today, have never been found.

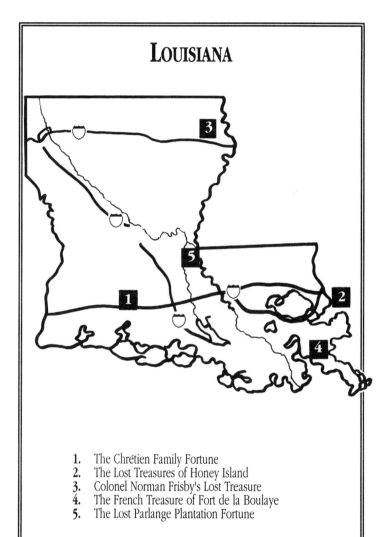

LOUISIANA

1. The Chrétien Family Fortune
2. The Lost Treasures of Honey Island
3. Colonel Norman Frisby's Lost Treasure
4. The French Treasure of Fort de la Boulaye
5. The Lost Parlange Plantation Fortune

The Chrétien
Family Fortune

A few years after the end of the War of 1812, Hippolyte Chrétien II, a member of Louisiana's plantation gentry and heir to his father's vast fortune, buried around half a million dollars in gold and silver coins and jewelry on his property. According to historical sources, the hidden trove was never retrieved, and there is strong evidence that it still lies buried deep below the surface of the bank of a bayou that can be seen from the second floor window of the aged and crumbling Chrétien mansion.

The Chrétien family had settled in Louisiana in the year 1776. Three brothers, Hippolyte, Jules, and Dazincourt, arrived from France seeking opportunities in agriculture and banking. They engaged in many successful ventures, among them the acquisition of a large cotton plantation located between Opelousas and Lafayette in southern Louisiana.

Hippolyte, always a bit more adventurous than his brothers, fell in with the notorious pirate Jean Lafitte and became involved in slave trading and piracy. On several occasions, Hippolyte allowed stolen slaves and contraband to be hidden on the plantation grounds. For this and other activities, he was paid generously by Lafitte.

When Lafitte and members of his band joined General Andrew Jackson during the War of 1812, Hippolyte

Chrétien marched along beside them. While soldiering, he met and became good friends with a Spaniard named Neda, and when the war was over and Lafitte went on to other adventures, Chrétien and Neda returned to the cotton plantation, where together they transformed it into a hugely profitable success which made incredibly wealthy men of them.

Chrétien and Neda both had large families, and as the years passed, their respective children, Hippolyte Chrétien II and Félicité Neda developed a fondness for one another, and eventually were married.

The pair seemed ill-suited to one another: Chrétien was an overweight, shiftless, and timid young man with a penchant for drinking wine and counting his inheritance; Félicité was a spirited young lady who exercised a firm hand both in riding her horses and in running her portion of the plantation's affairs.

The newlyweds had constructed a modest home on the Chrétien plantation not far from the main house. For a time the marriage went smoothly, but over the years disagreements sprang up often and sometimes grew into violent arguments. Félicité wished to have a greater influence in the operation of the plantation, but Chrétien preferred that she assume the more traditional role of subservient housewife.

During this time, many plantation owners and other businessmen were leery of investing their money in banks, opting instead to hide it in secret locations on their property. Chrétien was no exception. In addition to his own share of the profits from the cotton plantation, Chrétien had inherited his father's fortune when the old man passed away. He decided to find a place where his wealth would be safe.

One day, while walking in a grove of trees adjacent to a bayou some eighty yards from his home, Hippolyte selected a suitable location in which to bury his fortune. He summoned an old slave and ordered him to carry several chests filled with gold and silver coins, as well as fine jewelry, out to the grove. There, in the dark of night, the slave dug an extremely deep hole in which the treasure was deposited.

Félicité was astounded when Hippolyte informed her he had hidden the family wealth, but she became totally incensed when he refused to tell her the location. For weeks she pleaded with her husband to reveal the site of the buried treasure, but he stubbornly refused.

More years passed, the plantation thrived, and Hippolyte and Félicité decided to build a mansion on the grounds which would be more suitable to their status as successful and wealthy citizens of southern Louisiana. The mansion took more than four years to construct, and was admired by citizens for miles around. Hippolyte II was able to stand at the window of his second floor bedroom and look down on the grove of trees below, where his fortune was buried.

Along with their fortune, the couple's family also grew—by 1830, they had three children.

In 1834, Hippolyte Chrétien II came down with yellow fever and died within weeks. Though Félicité pleaded with him on his deathbed, he never revealed the location of the buried Chrétien fortune.

Félicité continued to operate the plantation and in the ensuing years she made great profits, rivaling the success of her late husband. But though she was financially secure, she never gave up the search for the family treasure.

One bright, moonlit evening as Félicité was preparing for bed, she looked out her bedroom window toward the bayou that extended for some distance behind the mansion. In the center of a grove of trees she spied several men moving around, some of them digging in the ground. Arming herself with two pistols, she rushed downstairs and out the door, advanced upon the group, and ordered them to leave immediately. In response, one of them menacingly approached her. Without hesitation, she fired one of the pistols, killing her attacker instantly.

At the sound of gunfire, several slaves came running from their quarters and chased the remaining intruders away. When Félicité wondered aloud what the men might have been doing in the grove of trees, an old slave stepped forward. She remembered the man as one of her husband's favorites, and asked him what he knew. The old man volunteered that the visitors might have been interested in the treasure that was buried nearby.

Félicité asked the slave to explain to her what he knew about the Chrétien treasure, but he refused. After being told by his mistress that she would shoot him on the spot unless he cooperated, the old man broke down, sobbing, and related the story of how he had helped Hippolyte II bury the family treasure. Pressed for details, he confessed that he couldn't remember exactly where the fortune was hidden, but that it was somewhere in the grove of trees.

The next day, Félicité ordered several slaves into the grove to search for the treasure, but nothing was found. On several other occasions, she personally supervised some digging in the area but to no avail.

Félicité Chrétien passed away shortly before the outbreak of the War Between the States and her son, Hippolyte Chrétien III, assumed control of the plantation. In 1863, the plantation was invaded by Union soldiers. Several structures, including the barn, a cotton gin, and a warehouse were destroyed, but the mansion was left standing, and Hippolyte III was allowed to resume operation of the farm.

Hippolyte Chrétien III heard the story of his father's buried treasure but never believed it. The plantation continued to earn huge profits, and this generation of Chrétiens proved to be far more interested in the business of making money than in chasing down obscure tales of treasure.

When Hippolyte III passed away, his son Jules inherited the estate. Jules was much like his great-grandfather, Hippolyte I. He possessed a strong sense of adventure, cared little for the details and discipline involved in running a large farm, and gradually sold off his share of the plantation.

For much of his life, Jules searched for the lost Chrétien fortune unsuccessfully.

Chrétien Point, the location of the once thriving plantation, lies between Opelousas and Lafayette, near the town of Sunset. Long since turned over to creditors, the site bears scant resemblance to the successful cotton operation of a century and a half earlier.

Historians are convinced that the huge Chrétien fortune in gold and silver coins and jewelry still lies buried somewhere in the grove of trees next to the shallow bayou that runs across the property behind the old mansion. The treasure is apparently well-hidden; many claim the reason it was never recovered is that it was buried several feet deep, somewhat beyond the depth a casual digger would undertake.

There are many who believe that modern, sophisticated electronic equipment might easily reveal the location of the Chrétien treasure—something that, to date, has never been used in the area. If located, the chests filled with gold and silver coins and jewelry would be worth in excess of two million dollars today.

The Lost Treasures
of Honey Island

In the entire state of Louisiana, there is no place that can equal Honey Island in lost treasure history and folklore. Since the early 1800s, this mysterious island in the middle of the Pearl River has attracted pirates, thieves, murderers, adventurers, and rogues of all types. Because of the extremely wild and forbidding environments found on the island, men have chosen to hide their fortunes there, knowing that few would dare enter to search for them.

The state of Louisiana is shaped somewhat like a boot, with the toe pointing toward the east and abutting Mississippi. While the Mississippi River forms the boundary between Louisiana and Mississippi along the eastern edge of the upper part of the boot, the Pearl River forms the boundary along the toe. A slow-moving, silt-laden river, the Pearl lazily makes its way from the headwaters near Jackson to the Gulf of Mexico, some 150 miles to the south. As the river approaches sea level near the Mississippi town of Picayune, its velocity is not sufficient to continue to effectively transport the heavy load of silt and sand it is carrying, and therefore a great deal of the sediment is deposited on the river bed. This process has gone on for thousands of years, and eventually caused the formation of Honey Island. The island is thirty miles long and five miles wide, a narrow strip of land in the middle of the Pearl

River. The island has been described as a densely forested swampy lowland, crisscrossed by bayous and resembling a subtropical forest of mostly virgin timber, with a fork of the Pearl River flowing along either side of it.

For years it remained unclear whether the island was the property of Louisiana or Mississippi, and for a time both states claimed it, though neither bothered to survey or explore it. In fact, because of its wild nature and nearly impenetrable interior, the island was generally avoided by both states until the federal government entered the controversy several years later and formally made it part of Louisiana.

Because Honey Island had been ignored for so long, it became a kind of no man's land, attracting the likes of pirates, outlaws, and other ne'er-do-wells.

Among the earliest pirates to use Honey Island as a stronghold was Pierre Rameau. Rameau was one of several aliases used by Kirk McCollough, the son of an Irish minister who turned to piracy at an early age. Employing Honey Island as a base of operations, Rameau launched his ships from a point near the southern end and sent them into the Gulf of Mexico to attack and pillage merchant vessels.

Rameau also controlled a gang of land pirates which he dispatched into the settled areas of Louisiana and Mississippi to steal horses and cattle, rob banks, and conduct raids on isolated farmhouses.

So successful was Rameau that in a short time he had a warehouse constructed on Honey Island to store the booty from his outlaw operations on land and sea, which over the years had swollen to millions of dollars' worth. In addition to the goods stored in the warehouse, Rameau and a few of his most trusted men loaded hundreds of thousands of dollars' worth of gold coins into trunks and buried them at secret locations along the shore on the southern part of the island.

For reasons more political than patriotic, Rameau decided to align himself and a contingent of his men with General Andrew Jackson during the War of 1812. At the Battle of New Orleans, however, Rameau learned that the British forces far outnumbered Jackson's, and wanting always to be on the winning side of any battle, switched his allegiance to the British.

The move turned out to be an unfortunate one for Rameau, for Jackson's army soundly defeated the British troops, and Rameau himself was killed at the town of Chalmette during the fighting.

Following Rameau's death, many of his followers returned to Honey Island and helped themselves to most of the goods stored in the warehouse, but none were left alive who knew of the locations of the buried chests filled with gold coins.

Though it has never been proven that either of them ever belonged to Rameau, two gold-filled chests were found many years later. In 1907, a small group of hunters discovered one such chest containing just over one million dollars in gold coins. In 1912, while exploring along the eastern shore of the island across the river from Pearlington, Mississippi, a fisherman came across a heavy chain attached to a large tree. The other end of the chain was buried in the sand, and the curious fisherman decided to investigate. Digging a five-foot-deep hole, he found a large chest secured to the other end of the chain. The chest was completely filled with gold coins.

During the 1820s, notorious outlaw John Murrell also used Honey Island as a base of operations. His gang, which was said to have numbered well over a hundred men, brought the spoils of their raids to the island to be hidden in several huge caches which Murrell had established over the years. When Murrell added to one of the caches, he did so with the help of only one man, a trusted friend, and only the two of them knew the secret locations of the hidden wealth.

During a midnight crossing of the Pearl River, Murrell's friend accidentally slipped overboard and drowned. Several weeks later, Murrell himself was imprisoned. After his death, no one knew the location of the secret caches.

Two decades later, the daring highwayman James Copeland and his gang took up residence on Honey Island. Copeland was a colorful, good-humored bandit who conducted raids as far east as Alabama and as far west as south-central Texas.

It was never known how much wealth Copeland accumulated, but the spoils of his raids were always returned to Honey Island and buried there.

The daring bandit began to attract the attention of numerous lawmen, and soon much of the South was searching for him. As the reward money offered for his capture grew to impressive amounts, one of his own henchmen eventually turned him in. After a lengthy trial, Copeland was declared guilty and sentenced to be hanged. A few days before his scheduled execution, he dictated a brief summary of his exploits to Dr. J.R.S. Pitts, the sheriff of Perry County, Mississippi. The transcript contained an inventory of Copeland's robberies and close estimates of the total amount of money taken during each one. Copeland also related that most of the loot was buried on Honey Island, and as well as he could, he provided descriptions of and directions to the burial sites.

On October 30, 1857, James Copeland was executed on the gallows at Old Augusta, Mississippi. Several days later the transcript was made public and dozens of treasure hunters swarmed to Honey Island, lured by the buried treasures. Some small amount of Copeland's loot was retrieved, but most of it remained hidden from the searchers.

Following the War Between the States, bands of men spurred on by bitterness, hatred, greed, and the lust for adventure roamed the countryside, raiding farms, robbing banks, and often killing innocent citizens. Such men were called jayhawkers, and residents on both sides of the Mason-Dixon Line lived in fear of them.

The Civil War had just ended when one such band of jayhawkers systematically preyed upon the small towns and farms along the Pearl River in south-central Mississippi. While looting one small river town, the bandits boarded and comandeered an eighty-foot sailing vessel named the *Delta*. Deciding to make their getaway via the river instead of by land, the inexperienced crew of outlaws pushed off from the shore, hoisted sails, and managed to point the boat downstream.

As they sailed down the Pearl, the jayhawkers put to shore at every opportunity to raid small river port towns, strip homes of valuables, and rob citizens in the streets. Over the course of a week, the bandits accumulated chests full of gold and silver coins, jewelry, and other goods, all of which they stored in the hold of the ship.

Unknown to the jayhawkers, several bands of their now irate, vengeance-minded victims had formed vigilante groups and had set off downriver in boats, hoping to overtake the outlaws and reclaim their stolen goods. By the time the bandits steered their captured vessel to the waters of the east fork of the Pearl River, the pursuers had traveled to within a few hundred yards of the *Delta*. Neither the jayhawkers nor the vigilantes were experienced sailors, and the chase became almost laughable, with quarry and hunters alike getting snagged on sandbars and running into the shore. Gradually, however, the vigilantes gained on the outlaws.

One afternoon, as the jayhawkers taunted their pursuers, the *Delta* struck a large submerged tree trunk, went out of control, and slammed onto the shore of Honey Island. The vessel was destroyed, and the outlaws, unable to continue their flight, hurriedly began to unload the booty from the boat and bury it at several locations near the shore. Just as they finished concealing about half of the loot, the first of the pursuers landed on the island and a violent gun battle erupted. The outlaws, now in a panic, fled into the swampy, vegetation-choked interior of Honey Island. Before fleeing, however, they set the *Delta* on fire.

As the vessel burned, the vigilantes fired after the fleeing bandits, killing several of them. Three of the outlaws were eventually captured, executed on the spot, and buried in a common grave.

The vigilantes, believing that all of the stolen loot was still on board the *Delta,* next turned their attention to the burning ship. As they attempted to extinguish the fire, the vessel shifted, drifted out onto the river, and sank in relatively shallow water not far from the shore.

The gold and silver coins, along with a considerable amount of jewelry, guns, and valuable artifacts, were never found. The vigilantes were unaware that most of the coins and jewelry had been removed from the ship and buried on the island. The remainder of the treasure on board the *Delta* settled onto the gravel bottom of the east fork of the Pearl River, where it remains to this day.

Today Honey Island is considerably more accessible than it was a hundred years ago. It can be crossed using Interstate 59, but travel to the remote parts of the interior must be made on foot through forbidding, swampy lowlands infested with snakes and insects.

Most of the island is now owned by a paper company which is in the business of timber cutting and experimental reforestation. A few small, poor farms dot the remainder of the area.

In spite of the many attempts made to locate the hidden treasures of Rameau, Murrell, Copeland, and the jayhawkers, most of their lost wealth remains buried beneath the ancient river silt that makes up Honey Island.

Colonel Norman Frisby's Lost Treasure

For a period of some ten years prior to the War Between the States, Colonel Norman Frisby was one of the most successful and best-known plantation owners in the South. His farm, which consisted of 42,000 acres stretched along the Tensas River in northeastern Louisiana for twenty-five miles, was a model of agricultural efficiency and productivity for the time. According to historians, Frisby was the largest slaveholder in America, possessing more than 500.

The life of Colonel Frisby was shrouded in mystery and punctuated by extreme notoriety and widespread suspicion of piracy. Alternately praised as a progressive plantation owner and condemned as a cruel master to his slaves, Frisby quietly amassed a fortune. As the Civil War became imminent, Frisby considered his fortune in jeopardy and had it buried in the dense marshlands near his mansion. To this day the great Frisby treasure has not been recovered.

It was never clear where Norman Frisby came from. Sometime during the mid-1850s, he appeared at a Mississippi plantation owned by his uncle. The uncle hired Frisby to oversee the plantation, and under the newcomer's supervision cotton farming proceeded more efficiently than ever before, though his methods were sometimes questioned. Frisby believed success resulted from hard work, in particular the hard work of the slaves. He ran the plantation with an iron hand, riding horseback across his holdings from dawn until midnight, constantly and harshly whipping and driving the slaves.

Frisby had swamps drained and forests cleared and grew cotton where it had never grown before. He doubled the number of slaves in the field and kept them constantly attending the crop to the point that nearly twice as many bales of cotton per acre were produced than in previous years. More cotton translated into greater profits, and Frisby and the uncle grew richer with each passing year.

No one knows where Frisby acquired the title of colonel. There is no record of his service in the United States military and many believe he simply bestowed it upon himself. Nevertheless, he came to be known as "the colonel" in Mississippi and Louisiana, and the name stayed with him for the rest of his life.

For a half-dozen years Frisby managed his uncle's plantation. Impressed with the great profits that could be made from the growing and selling of cotton, Frisby decided in 1861 to purchase a plantation of his own. After spending several months searching, he located and purchased thousands of acres of rich bottomland in the Tensas River Basin in northeastern Louisiana near the present-day town of Newlight. It remains unclear how Frisby managed to acquire enough money to purchase such a large plantation, for the price far exceeded the wages he earned while working on his uncle's farm. It was widely rumored that Frisby had been a pirate before his arrival at the Mississippi plantation, and many believed he brought the spoils of numerous raids when he retired from the open seas and fled to Mississippi. Others claimed he discovered some of pirate Jean Lafitte's buried treasure. At any rate, by the time Frisby purchased the land he was already a wealthy man.

As in Mississippi, Frisby worked his slaves mercilessly on the new plantation, and the result was a bountiful crop the first year and an increasingly efficient operation each year thereafter, even more successful than that of his uncle.

Stories abound of Frisby's treatment of his slaves. Their hours were long, and Frisby sometimes withheld food or water from them during the hot and humid summer days in the Louisiana bottomlands. Slaves often died in the field and their bodies were dragged away while the others were whipped into continuing to work.

As Frisby's plantation thrived, he took a wife who bore him two daughters during the following two years. While Frisby and his family lived in a three-room cabin near the river, he initiated construction of an extravagant thirty-room mansion on the highest elevation of the plantation. Frisby's new home was intended to be the biggest and showiest residence in the South. While the mansion was being built, the colonel purchased numerous fixtures for it such as pure gold and silver doorknobs, silver window frames, and gold light fixtures. At the request of his wife he ordered gold dinnerware. The crowning touch was a huge silver bell that weighed approximately 200 pounds. Frisby himself transported several bags filled with silver dollars to New York and had them melted down and fashioned into the bell, which was to be hung in front of the house to announce visitors to the plantation. Neighboring plantation owners possessed similar bells, but none as large, splendid, and pretentious as this one.

While Frisby's plantation prospered and the colonel grew even more wealthy, he was never completely accepted into social life as it existed in that part of Louisiana. Exclusion from the society circles bothered Frisby deeply, and he soon came to resent his neighbors. Many of them avoided the colonel because of his brutal treatment of his slaves. Though all plantation owners possessed slaves, none were as vicious in dealing with them as was the colonel. It is said that during the time he owned his Tensas River plantation, Frisby filled a cemetery with slaves who died from overwork in the fields or from starvation.

Growing ever more arrogant and haughty, Frisby found himself actually shunned by his neighbors. The ostracization infuriated the colonel, and his relationships with plantation owners up and down the river became more strained with each passing week.

Frisby's nearest neighbor was a man named Flowers who also happened to be his brother-in-law. Flowers owned several mules that he allowed to wander around unfenced. Occasionally Frisby encountered one or more of Flowers's mules munching the tender tops of the young cotton plants in his fields. Normally Frisby would herd the mules back to Flowers's corral and caution the man about letting the animals run loose.

One morning while surveying his domain on horseback, Frisby encountered two of Flowers's mules grazing along the rows of his cotton field. Enraged by the repeated transgressions, Frisby shot both of them.

With his anger building, the colonel rode straight to Flowers's house. On arriving, he called him out and cursed him in front of his wife and children. Flowers pulled a pistol from a sash he wore around his mid-section, leveled it at Frisby, and ordered him off his land, telling him if he ever returned he would be killed. Frisby turned his horse and rode away, swearing revenge on his wife's brother.

As the weeks and months passed, Frisby took his anger out on his slaves, working and whipping them harder than ever. Several of them escaped and sought refuge at other plantations where they related the horrors of the colonel's punishments.

More time passed, and rumors of war arrived in northeastern Louisiana. In addition, a bill designed to outlaw slavery in the state was being submitted to the legislature. The bill was drafted in part as a response to Colonel Frisby's treatment of his slaves.

With these unsettling prospects at hand, Frisby decided to transport most of his slaves to Texas, where he knew he would be able to sell them and make a good profit. When the colonel returned to his plantation several weeks later and 270,000 dollars in gold coins richer, he was greeted with the news that war was imminent. Concerned that his wealth would be seized should Louisiana be invaded by Union troops, Frisby ordered two of his remaining slaves to load into a wagon all the gold and silver fixtures awaiting installation in the mansion still under construction. In a second wagon, Frisby loaded the solid silver bell and the 270,000 dollars in gold coins along with at least two kegs filled with silver coins which he unearthed near his cabin.

Taking command of one of the wagons, Frisby directed the slaves to follow in the other as he drove into the dense marshland located near the margin of his property. Once in the swampy lowlands, the trail disappeared and the heavily-loaded wagons labored through the soft, mushy soil. When they could continue no farther, Frisby ordered the slaves to unload everything from the wagons and bury it on the spot. A huge hole was excavated, and into it were deposited the gold coins, the kegs, the bell, and all of the gold and silver fixtures, ornaments, and dinnerware once destined for the fine mansion.

When the two slaves finally covered over the hole, Frisby asked them both if they thought they could ever find this location again. One of the slaves thought he couldn't but the other nodded that he could. Frisby immediately grabbed this slave and, with a sudden movement, broke his neck and flung the body atop the recently filled hole. Frisby, driving one of the wagons, led the way out of the marsh. He was followed by the terrified surviving slave driving the second wagon.

On the way back to the mansion, Frisby noticed one of Flowers's mules grazing in his cotton field. Furious, he reached into the back of the wagon, seized his rifle, and shot the animal. Deciding once and for all to settle with Flowers, Frisby ordered the slave to return the second wagon to the plantation headquarters while he set out for Flowers's home.

The frightened slave, ignoring Frisby's order, drove the wagon directly to his shack, quickly loaded up his family and a few belongings, and fled to Texas that same afternoon. Colonel Frisby and the slave were the only two living souls who knew where the treasure was buried, and the slave was never seen again.

On arriving at Flowers's home, Frisby was informed by the housekeeper that the entire family was attending a community picnic at Flowers Landing on the Tensas River. Further enraged that he and his family had not been invited to the gathering, Frisby angrily lashed his weary horse toward the landing.

Into the midst of the fun and gaiety of the picnic Frisby steered the wagon, cursing Flowers at the top of his lungs. Spotting the object of his ire among the crowd, Frisby seized his whip and attacked the smaller man, laying lash after lash upon his back. Flowers was able to grab the whip and pull Frisby toward him. At the same time, he seized a long knife which he had just used to carve some meat, and plunged it repeatedly into Frisby's chest.

Frisby collapsed to the ground, dead, and with him went the secret of the location of his buried fortune.

The War Between the States came and went and much of the South changed. The old plantations were no longer able to operate as before, and many of them had to be abandoned altogether. Today, little remains of the uncompleted Frisby mansion. The land that was once the prosperous Frisby plantation has gone through a succession of owners but it is still regarded as valuable farmland and each year yields a healthy crop.

Out on the margins of this farmland remain areas of marshland, and within one of these cottonmouth- and mosquito-infested lowlands lies well over a million dollars' worth of gold and silver still buried in the dark soil, a fortune waiting to be recovered.

The French Treasure
of Fort de la Boulaye

In 1698, King Louis XIV ordered his soldiers to occupy the Louisiana territory and claim it in the name of France. Along with the military, the king sent cartographers to map the lower Mississippi River and gulf coast, and Jesuit priests to convert the Indians to Christianity. In order to facilitate trade and to pay the members of the expedition, the French government provided them with 160,000 dollars in gold and silver coins. Louis also financed several other expeditions into the region in order to learn more about the culture of the Indians and the natural resources of the area—information which would help him to evaluate the possibilities for increased trade and settlement in the New World.

Because the British also had designs on the area, Louis ordered a series of forts constructed along the great river to defend the region against the English threat.

Leading one of the earliest expeditions up the river was Pierre Le Moyne Sieur d'Iberville. With four ships and approximately seventy men, d'Iberville crossed the Atlantic Ocean and traveled to a point near Biloxi, Mississippi, where he landed and established a temporary settlement. Leaving several men to maintain the small encampment, d'Iberville took three of the ships and sailed to the mouth of the Mississippi River. After waiting three days for the winds to change direction, d'Iberville was finally able to sail upstream. For nearly two weeks he searched for a suitable location for a fort and a new settlement, but everywhere he looked he found nothing but low-lying swampland. Discouraged and unable to decide on an appropriate site, d'Iberville ordered the vessels to return to Biloxi.

Several months later, d'Iberville once again set sail up the Mississippi River, and eventually decided on a location on the highest ground he could find. Only about two feet above the level of the stream, the river bank location was an excellent position from which to prevent the passage of the British vessels up the river. The site was near the present-day town of Phoenix.

Using the abundant cane which grew along the shore, the Frenchmen immediately began building shelters and a magazine.

While the construction continued, d'Iberville led a band of men upstream, where they felled dozens of cypress trees and floated them down to the new colony.

Gradually, Fort de la Boulaye and the adjoining colony took shape. The main building was a two-story structure, twenty-eight feet square, built entirely of cypress logs, and crowned by a quartet of four-pound guns and two eighteen-pound cannons. As the adjacent banks and forests were being cleared in anticipation of arriving settlers, this log fortress stood guard over the river. The fort and the French vessels patrolling this portion of the Mississippi River made passage by British ships virtually impossible, and the French maintained domination over the region.

On those occasions when the British did manage to get this far upstream, the French would intercept them and explain that the entire river was rife with forts, and that to continue was foolhardy. In each case, the captain of the British ship ordered the vessel to return to the gulf. To this day, this stretch of the Mississippi River is still referred to as the English Turn.

Soon after the main building and magazine were constructed, d'Iberville left Fort de la Boulaye to explore the farther reaches of the river. In his absence, work progressed slowly, and the citizens of the new colony were repeatedly visited by violent storms. Hurricanes of great intensity and duration frequently flooded the area; it often took several weeks for the floodwaters to recede. When strong winds blew from the south, which they did often, the waters were driven onto the low-lying land, again flooding the entire colony. High winds often destroyed the flimsy cane structures, leaving residents without shelter. After a few years, the situation became unbearable, and the citizens of Fort de la Boulaye decided to abandon the area and sail back to Biloxi.

Before departing on his extended explorations, d'Iberville had left one of the ships in the small river harbor for use by the residents, but it had been sunk during one of the violent storms. Word was sent to the settlement at Biloxi requesting another ship to evacuate citizens from the area, but when it did not arrive in a reasonable amount of time, they decided to abandon the colony and strike out on foot.

Packing only survival necessities for the long journey to the Mississippi coast, the colonists left behind many useful items. The 160,000 dollars in gold and silver coins, along with additional monies which had been brought to the colony, was much too heavy to transport across the marshy bottomlands of the delta. The coins were placed in two large wooden chests and buried. Some researchers claim the treasure was buried in the dirt floor of the log fortress, while others support the notion that it was buried in a community garden.

Though the French intended to return someday to Fort de la Boulaye to reoccupy it and recover the treasure, growing problems with the Indians and the British prevented them from doing so.

Years passed, and storms and floods destroyed much of what was left of the unoccupied fort. In time, the tenacious swamp vegetation reclaimed the cleared settlement and enveloped the structures, including the cypress log fortress. After many years in the hot steamy swamplands, most of the buildings rotted away.

Sometime during the mid-1700s, the Mississippi River shifted its course as the result of a severe flood, and a new channel was cut nearly a quarter of a mile away, leaving the old fort isolated and out of the view of travelers. Subsequent expeditions in search of the fort were fruitless, and its actual location became a mystery. The two chests containing the fortune in gold and silver coins reposed in the ground, no doubt decaying like the old structures of the long abandoned settlement.

Fort de la Boulaye soon disappeared from even the collective memory of the French, the records of its existence buried in obscure histories and in a musty old journal that was kept by one of the Jesuits originally assigned to d'Iberville.

Around 1900, interest in Fort de la Boulaye was revived and historians searched throughout the Mississippi Delta for its remains. Though this activity continued for a period three years, no evidence of the old fort was found.

Then, in 1932, construction workers were digging a canal in order to drain a portion of the huge swamp adjacent to the river when they encountered several old, hand-hewn cypress logs under a heavy layer of silt. When researchers heard of the discovery, they descended on the area and undertook a careful study of the items they found. After examining the remains, the investigators determined that the site was, in fact, that of the long-lost Fort de la Boulaye.

Among the remains were remnants of the old cypress log building, several items of rolled sheet metal, tools, cannon balls, and several gold coins.

Many have traveled to the fort in an attempt to locate the chests filled with gold and silver coins, estimated to be worth well over one million dollars today. The search has been difficult, for no one is exactly certain where the chests were buried. An excavation of the floor of the old fort yielded nothing, and the location of the community garden relative to the log building is unknown.

Further impeding efforts to recover the treasure is the harsh and often dangerous swampland, replete with poisonous snakes, treacherous quicksand, annoying insects, extreme heat, stifling humidity, and the ever-encroaching vegetation.

That the treasure is still there, buried deep in the silt of the former river bank, is certain, though some have suggested that the weight of the coins has caused them to sink deeper into the loosely consolidated soil.

The search continues today, and the site of old Fort de la Boulaye is visited often by fortune hunters who believe they will be the ones to find the French treasure. The location of the gold and silver coins, like the fort itself at one time, remains a mystery. As a result of pure chance, the fort was rediscovered. Perhaps in the same way the treasure will be found as well.

The Lost Parlange Plantation Fortune

Madame Virginie Parlange was a wealthy widow who owned and managed the great Parlange plantation near the town of New Roads, Louisiana, at the time of the War Between the States.

When word reached Madame Parlange that Union troops were approaching, she immediately made plans to hide her fortune as well as many priceless domestic furnishings. After gathering up her finest silver, china, and jewelry, she removed several wallboards, stuffed her treasured belongings into the spaces between the inside and outside walls, and then refastened the planks. She had her best furniture carried up to the spacious attic and covered with quilts.

The Parlange fortune, estimated at between a third and a half of a million dollars in gold and silver coins, was placed in three massive wooden chests. Madame Parlange ordered two of her most trusted servants to drag the chests out to the garden, where they were hastily buried.

This done, Madame Parlange returned to her stately mansion and calmly awaited the arrival of the Union forces.

Soon enough, Yankee soldiers rode into the great yard of the Parlange plantation. The impressive home, which had been constructed by the Marquis Vincent de Ternant in 1750, was surrounded by groves of live oak and pecan trees, and beyond that, as far as the eye could see, were vast fields of sugar cane.

Madame Parlange came out on the front porch of the mansion and greeted the soldiers, even inviting them to dinner. The Yankee officers treated the old woman with kindness, camped on her property for a few days, and then left.

Fearful that other Union squads might arrive at the plantation, Madame Parlange decided to leave the family treasures hidden until the war was over.

Finally, when it became clear that the hostilities were drawing to a close, Madame Parlange, with the help of her son, Charles, began working to restore the plantation to its former glory. The furniture and expensive rugs that had been stored in the attic were carried down and returned to their former positions in the large rooms. The silver, china, and jewelry were removed from between the walls, cleaned, and placed in use once again.

When it came time to dig up the three chests of gold and silver coins, Madame Parlange led her son out to the garden and told him where to dig the first hole. Within minutes, the first chest was removed and carried into the mansion. A few yards away, a second chest was unearthed and taken inside. But when Madame Parlange directed Charles to dig at a certain location for the third and final chest, he found nothing. Several other excavations were made in the area, to no avail. For several days the two continued to examine the garden and dug more holes, completely ruining the garden, but still the chest eluded them.

When Madame Parlange summoned the two slaves who had helped her bury the three chests, they could not be found. She learned later that they had escaped to Texas.

After the war was over, the Parlange plantation fell upon hard times. Without the slaves, it was difficult to harvest the sugar cane. Charles, who never cared much for farming anyway, went away to law school. Years later he was appointed a justice of the Supreme Court of Louisiana.

When Madame Parlange passed away, the mansion remained empty for nearly twenty years. Walter Parlange, son of Charles and grandson of Madame, took control of the plantation in 1923 and attempted to restore it to prosperity.

It was only after Walter had lived on the plantation for many years that he heard the story of the buried treasure. Using family documents, Walter Parlange estimated that the lost chest contained at least 100,000 dollars at 1860 values. Today, of course, the contents of the chest would be worth considerably more.

Walter undertook several searches for the missing treasure, but was unable even to identify the location of the old garden. Eventually he gave up any hope of finding the chest.

During the 1950s, several groups of treasure hunters were allowed onto the property to attempt to locate the buried chest. While several systematic searches were undertaken, none of them were successful.

According to members of the Parlange family, the chest containing a fortune in gold and silver coins is still buried somewhere on the plantation in the vicinity of the old mansion.

MISSISSIPPI

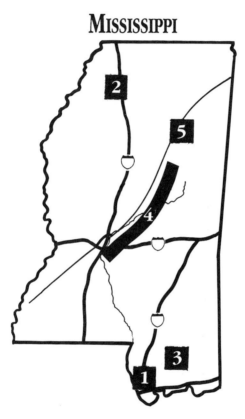

1. The Lost Bonaparte Treasure
2. Lost Train Robbery Gold
3. Pirate Captain's Buried Gold
4. The Natchez Trace: Mississippi Treasure Trail
5. Lost Chest of Gold Coins of Choctaw County

The Lost Bonaparte Treasure

In 1815, following his defeat at Waterloo, Napoleon Bonaparte was confined to a small, filthy jail cell on the remote South Atlantic island of St. Helena (now called Ascension Island). Soon afterwards, several groups developed plans to free the former emperor and return him to his previous glory. Most of these groups gradually dissolved, but one, headed by Napoleon's brother, Jerome Bonaparte, king of Westphalia, was determined to raise a force, take the island, and return Napoleon to the throne.

To that end, Jerome traveled throughout Europe and North America in an attempt to raise money to pay for a small army. Aided by a cadre of loyal Frenchmen, Jerome planned to liberate his brother and establish a new empire for him in Louisiana. He decided to travel to New Orleans, which had a large French population, to attract sympathizers, raise funds, and initiate preparations for establishing New France.

Because of the clandestine nature of his activities, Jerome left France in an ordinary merchant ship so as not to attract attention. Accompanying him were several French sailors and soldiers loyal to the deposed emperor. Jerome's baggage included a large wooden chest containing approximately 80,000 dollars' worth of gold, to be used for recruitment and the purchase of materials as well as to pay his followers.

There were numerous pirates who frequented the Gulf of Mexico, so Jerome's vessel sailed close to the coast and only at night in order to escape detection. As if the pirates weren't danger enough, there were others in the area who were hostile to Napoleon and aware of Jerome's plans to liberate him. Jerome knew they would do all they could to thwart him and steal his fortune.

Anticipating that their enemies might be waiting for them at the port of New Orleans, Jerome's guides arranged for a landing near what is now Waveland, Mississippi. Their intention was to travel overland and arrive at the Crescent City unnoticed. Meeting Jerome at the Mississippi landing was one Jeremiah Henley, a former mercenary who had aided Napoleon during the fight with Russia, and who was sympathetic to the plans for liberating the imprisoned leader.

After spending several days resting and making preparations in the Waveland area, Henley and several of the French soldiers loaded the supplies and gold onto horses and began their journey to New Orleans. On arriving at the east fork of the Pearl River, the boundary between southern Mississippi and Louisiana, the party set up camp some distance from the shore and made plans to cross the wide, muddy expanse in the morning.

While preparing a meal in camp, the party was alerted by one of the scouts that numerous bandit gangs had been seen along the route to New Orleans. Apparently, the news of Jerome's arrival and of the presence of the gold was already known by many. Fearful of losing the fortune to outlaws, Jerome, with the help of two soldiers, carried the chest of gold to a location approximately 1,000 feet from the east fork of the Pearl River and buried it. The site was described as being filled with a thick, dense growth of oak trees and understory vegetation. Fearful that even some of his own followers might be contemplating stealing the treasure, Jerome returned to the site during the night, excavatcd the chest, and reburied it about twenty yards away.

In the morning, the party, led by Henley, crossed the river and proceeded on to New Orleans. The treasure-filled chest remained behind in the secret location known only to Jerome.

Along the way, the small party was approached several times by bandits, but because the Frenchmen had disguised themselves as poor travelers, they were left alone. Once, when warned of an approaching gang of cutthroats, the party fled into the shelter of the dense vegetation alongside the trail.

There they remained for several hours as the bandits set up a temporary camp alongside the path the Frenchmen had just quit. Finally, the outlaws left the area and the would-be liberators, after enduring mosquitoes, heat, humidity, and snakes, were finally able to proceed on to New Orleans.

Upon his arrival, Jerome was received warmly by French sympathizers. After explaining his plan to free his brother, however, he learned that most of them were not willing to invest any time, energy, money, or even man-power on what they considered to be a foolish venture. While Jerome was invited to remain in New Orleans as long as he cared to, he felt unwelcome, and began to make plans to return to Waveland.

On the morning of his scheduled departure, Henley learned that more bandits had become aware of Jerome's presence in the city, and presuming he was traveling with the chest filled with gold, were lying in wait along the route back to Mississippi. Fearing for their lives, Jerome, Henley, and the others opted to leave via ship. Boarding a vessel at the New Orleans port, the group sailed without incident out into the gulf, crossed the Atlantic, and eventually arrived in France. Because of political and economic considerations, they were never able to return to Mississippi and the Pearl River to retrieve the buried chest of gold.

Several years later, a small settlement was established near the spot where Jerome had buried the gold. In honor of the former emperor, the settlement was named Napoleon.

Somewhere near the long-abandoned settlement, approximately 1,000 yards from the east fork of the Pearl River, lies an incredible fortune in gold in a wooden chest buried several inches below the surface.

Lost Train Robbery Gold

During the early part of the twentieth century, railroads were often the lifeblood of scattered and remote geographic regions and small communities, their tracks linking the small rural areas with the large commercial centers of the Midwest and the East. During this time, northern Mississippi had settled into a comfortable and relatively successful pattern of crop agriculture, based on cotton. The railroads often carried the bales of cotton to the northern and eastern markets and returned with goods otherwise unavailable in the sparsely settled parts of the South.

The Illinois Central Railroad wound through a portion of Mississippi, carrying passengers, freight, mail, and supplies to the Southerners. In addition, the trains often carried payrolls of cash, gold, and silver.

On the morning of April 21, 1909, an employee of llinois Central named Charlie Bowman was working with a track repair crew near Water Valley, a small north-central Mississippi town located in Yalobusha County. During a break, Bowman heard several men talking about a gold shipment that was being transported by the railroad. No one was certain of the value of the cargo, but one of the men stated that the gold completely filled a large metal strongbox. The train carrying the gold was scheduled to pass down the line in a week.

Bowman, intrigued by the gold shipment, began to make plans to steal it. Enlisting two friends—James B. Cartwright and Bob Tyson—Bowman proposed a scheme to take the strongbox from the train. On the morning of April 29, the three men boarded the southbound Illinois Central at Taylor, a town some ten miles north of Water Valley in Lafayette County.

Sitting nervously among the passengers, the three men waited until the train was about two miles out of Taylor. At that point, one of the men approached the conductor and held a gun to his forehead. While another cautioned the passengers to remain calm, Bowman made his way to the engine and threatened to kill the engineer if he did not stop the train.

Once the train was halted, the gold-filled metal strongbox was dumped beside the tracks. Waving their guns at the engineer, the men ordered the train to continue on to Water Valley.

Unprepared for the great weight of the strongbox, the three men struggled to alternately carry and drag it to a nearby bridge which crossed the tracks. Unable to break into the strongbox and unwilling to transport it on foot much farther, the men decided to bury it and return for it later when things cooled down. With difficulty, they dragged the box to a location about one hundred feet west of the bridge, excavated a hole, and buried it. After filling the hole, they noted three large oak trees near the site of the cache, and felt certain they could easily return to the site in the future.

Tyson suggested the three of them flee to Arkansas. He had a sister living there, and said she would allow them to remain with her for awhile. On foot, the men set off on the long journey to Arkansas.

As soon as the train arrived at Water Valley, the local law enforcement authorities were informed of the robbery, and a small posse was dispatched on horseback to the scene of the crime. Because of the drag marks in the dirt caused by the heavy strongbox, the posse had little difficulty picking up the trail of the three men. Approximately four hours after the robbery, Bowman, Cartwright, and Tyson were overtaken by their trackers.

Not inclined to be arrested, the train robbers drew their guns, took shelter behind some trees, and began shooting at their pursuers. Within minutes, Bowman and Tyson were killed and Cartwright was captured.

Under questioning, Cartwright refused to reveal the location where the men had buried the strongbox. One of the posse members recalled the drag marks caused by the heavy chest, and claimed it would be an easy task to follow them and retrieve the gold. Unfortunately, a heavy rain fell that night, and the drag marks were washed away. Several posse members searched the area of the robbery for several hours the following day but were unable to find any tracks.

Cartwright maintained his silence, refusing to cooperate with law officers. He was subsequently charged with and found guilty of train robbery, and sentenced to twenty years in prison. Cartwright was determined to serve his sentence, try for an early parole, and return to the robbery scene to retrieve the gold.

Misfortune was to continue to dog Cartwright, however, and during his twelfth year of imprisonment he developed a severe case of tuberculosis. Doctors gave him only a few weeks to live. Discouraged, Cartwright sent for his brother Robert, a resident of Oxford, Mississippi.

As he lay dying on his prison cot, Cartwright related the particulars of the robbery of the gold shipment to his brother. He told of dragging the strongbox into the woods west of the bridge and burying it, and he provided his brother with information regarding local landmarks and the proximity of the three large oak trees to the cache. Two days later, James B. Cartwright died.

Robert Cartwright remained long enough to see to the burial of his brother. On returning to Oxford, he immediately made plans to travel to Lafayette County to search for the fortune in gold he knew was buried near the old bridge.

Arriving at the bridge several days later, Robert was dismayed to discover that a recent fire had destroyed the forest for miles around. The alteration of the environment left him confused, and he was unable to discern the landmarks described by his brother. He spent several hours trying to get his bearings west of the bridge, but the large trees noted by his brother were no longer there.

Robert became frustrated and soon quit the site, completely forgoing any future attempts at locating the treasure.

When Cartwright's story eventually became known to the public, several attempts were made to recover the buried treasure, but none were successful.

The old bridge site is easily accessible today, located where Highway 7 crosses the railroad tracks south of the town of Taylor. The area where the strongbox is thought to have been buried is now covered with second-growth timber and a thick tangle of underbrush.

Treasure hunters still come from time to time to this area, each believing that sophisticated metal-detecting equipment will help them locate the gold cache. To date it remains undiscovered.

Pirate Captain's Buried Gold

Somewhere not far from the town of Saucier in Harrison County, near a long-abandoned plantation, are buried three wooden chests filled with gold and jewels worth several million dollars. The treasure was stolen by a pirate known only as Dane, who later committed suicide rather than be taken by law enforcement officials.

The secret of the location of his fabulous wealth went with him to the grave.

This tale has its beginnings in the early 1800s in Montevideo, the capital city of Uruguay. Montevideo is across the Rio de la Plata estuary from Buenos Aires, Argentina. At this bustling South American port, the ship *Nightingale* had been docked for several days while it was being loaded with goods to be transported to New Orleans. During the final day of docking, passengers arrived with their trunks as the vessel was being readied for departure.

The captain of the *Nightingale* was Dane. He was only in his mid-twenties, which was young for a ship's captain, but he had previously distinguished himself on several voyages from Montevideo to a number of ports along the Gulf of Mexico. His skill at commanding a ship and handling a crew was outstanding, and demand for his services grew.

Among the bars and taverns of the low ports along the South American coast, Dane had another reputation—that of a pirate. Originally from England, Dane fell in with freebooters as a thirteen-year-old, and was involved in numerous plunders on the high seas. In a short time he became captain of his own pirate vessel, and conducted dozens of successful raids on coastal towns and unsuspecting freighters. Dane's luck ran out after a few years, when he was captured by the British, returned to England, and sentenced to hang for his crimes. Bribing a jailer, Dane managed to escape from England and flee to South America, where he found honest work freighting goods up and down the western Atlantic coast.

Though Dane earned a good living as captain of the *Nightingale,* he missed the adventurous life of the buccaneer, and longed to assemble a crew and return to the relatively easy and lucrative occupation of raiding on the high seas. However, he decided to wait a few years, until such time as the British authorities had forgotten him.

Among the passengers boarding the *Nightingale* for the United States was one Señor Vineiro, a wealthy plantation owner from Brazil, and his quite young and beautiful bride. Included in Vineiro's baggage was 200,000 dollars' worth of gold coins and jewelry.

Vineiro's wife was the comely daughter of a prominent Argentine rancher named Regalea, who had arranged the marriage. Although Vineiro was thirty years older than she and the two had little in common, Julia looked forward to the journey to Louisiana, where her new husband expected to establish and develop a large sugar plantation.

Shortly after coming on board, Julia became attracted to the dashing ship captain, and Dane made certain she was aware of his own interest in her. In the evening, when Vineiro would retire to his cabin, Julia would slip away to Dane's quarters. So enraptured was the young lady with Dane that she began contemplating leaving her new husband and running away with the former pirate when the ship reached New Orleans.

Julia's nighttime escapades with Dane became common knowledge among most of the ship's crew, and it was not long before Vineiro was apprised of the relationship. He angrily accosted Dane one morning and ordered him to stay away from his wife or he would kill him. Dane protested that he was obviously the victim of a serious misunderstanding, and assured Vineiro that his young wife meant no more to him than any other passenger on the *Nightingale*.

Early the next morning, Señor Vineiro's lifeless body was discovered on the foredeck, a long knife protruding from his chest. Julia, now growing fearful of Dane, accused him of the murder and threatened to report him to the authorities as soon as they reached port. In response, Dane had Julia locked in a small storeroom below deck. Following her incarceration, Dane ransacked the Vineiro stateroom, and discovered the wealth in gold and jewels packed into a large steamer trunk.

Seeing an opportunity to come into great wealth, Dane decided to scuttle the *Nightingale* and flee with the gold. Instead of docking at New Orleans, Dane had the ship anchored just off Pass Christian, a small fishing port on the Mississippi coast.

Selecting three of his most trusted crew members, Dane had Vineiro's gold and jewelry packed into three smaller wooden chests and loaded onto a rowboat under cover of darkness. Next, they cut the two other rowboats loose to drift away on the current. With the remainder of the crew sound asleep below deck and the beautiful Julia locked up in the storeroom, Dane set the *Nightingale* on fire and fled with his three companions.

Rowing toward the distant shore near Pass Christian, Dane and his companions watched as the *Nightingale* blazed furiously and then sank, carrying at least two dozen bodies to the sandy floor beneath the dark gulf waters.

The next morning Dane purchased horses and supplies, and after loading goods and gold onto the mounts, set out with his companions toward the north. After traveling for two and a half days, they arrived near present-day Saucier close to the Wolf River. Dane liked the looks of the land he found and decided to establish a plantation there. Hiring several locals, he supervised the construction of a fine home and at the same time saw to the preparation of several hundred acres of fertile bottomland.

While his new home was being built, Dane, with the help of one of the crew members, buried the chests of gold in a selected location on his new property.

Researchers have long argued about where Dane hid his treasure. One story relates that the gold was cached under a large oak tree located in the front yard of his new home. Another version of the tale claims that one night Dane and one of his crewmen buried the gold beneath the floorboards of the house. Still others claim the treasure was buried in a spot which Dane had selected for a garden. In each version of the tale, the house figures prominently.

During the first few weeks after their arrival at this site, two of Dane's crew members mysteriously disappeared. While overseeing some of the workers in the field, the remaining crew member discovered the body of one of his companions in a nearby swamp. Like Señor Veneiro, the sailor had a dagger protruding from his chest.

Fearful that he would be Dane's next victim, the crewman fled that evening to Pass Christian. The morning after his arrival in the small port, the seaman learned that several members of the community were still curious about the burning and sinking of the vessel in the gulf several weeks earlier. Deciding to seek revenge on his former captain, the seaman went to the local authorities and revealed Dane's role in the robbery, the murders of the Vineiros and the ship's crew, the scuttling of the *Nightingale,* and the burial of the Vineiro's gold on the plantation.

Over a period of two days, a large posse assembled and left Pass Christian for Dane's plantation. Somehow, Dane learned of the betrayal by his former crewman and of the approaching posse. Realizing there was no way to escape capture, the young pirate decided to take his own life. Securing a rope to one of the rafters in the frame of his house, he tied the other end around his neck and leaped from a railing. Moments later, the posse arrived and found him still swinging, a hint of a smile on his face.

For several hours the posse members searched the grounds for Dane's treasure, but found nothing. Believing that the crewman who informed them of Dane's crimes could lead them to the gold, they returned to Pass Christian with the intention of bringing him to the plantation to point out the location of the cache. On arriving in the port city, however, they found the crewman sick in bed with a high fever. Within a week he was dead.

Many have searched for Dane's treasure over the past 170 years, but with no success. The house Dane was constructing burned to the ground a few years after his death. As time passed and the southern Mississippi rains beat down on the area, all evidence of the location of the structure was obliterated.

Around 1860, a Pass Christian old-timer claimed to have had a dream that Dane's wooden chests of gold and jewels lay buried beneath the floor of the old house. With two friends, the man traveled to the old Dane plantation, but was unable to locate the home site.

The 200,000 dollars in gold and jewels hidden by Dane would be worth several million dollars today. As clues to the geographic location of the old Dane plantation and home have dimmed over the years, so have the chances of locating the treasure.

Perhaps someday a local farmer, out plowing his field one morning, will accidentally unearth one or more of the old gold-filled chests.

The Natchez Trace: Mississippi Treasure Trail

Two hundred years ago the Natchez Trace was one of the most well traveled roads in the country. Extending from the Mississippi River port of Natchez toward the northeast through Mississippi, Alabama, and Tennessee to Nashville, the trail accommodated travelers of all kinds—pioneers and politicians, peddlers and preachers, settlers and soldiers, ladies of high breeding and ladies of the night.

Originally an old Indian trail, the Natchez Trace wound through a dense wilderness that was homeland to the Choctaw and Chickasaw Indians. As a result of the increased traffic along the trace, daring and resourceful robbers began to view it as a route along which they could grow wealthy stealing from and often murdering the wayfarers. Because of the high incidence of robbery and killing along the route, it was often referred to as the Devil's Backbone.

The heavy use of the trace grew out of a need for Mississippi River flatboat men and others to return to the North. When flatboats and barges carrying goods and passengers reached Natchez, the vessels were often cut up for firewood, as a return trip upriver against the strong current was all but impossible.

Many outlaws prospered along the trace, several of whom have gone down in history as notable villains.

Records attest that most of these outlaws buried great portions of their stolen money and goods at various points along the trace, caches that were often unclaimed and forgotten. It is estimated that millions of dollars' worth of gold and silver coins, jewelry, and artifacts are hidden adjacent to or near the Natchez Trace.

Two of the most notorious outlaws ever to prey on travelers along the trace were Samuel Mason and Wiley Harpe. Both men had practiced outlawry since they were children, both had served time in jail for their misdeeds, and both were wanted by the law for murder and robbery. Mason and Harpe found robbing travelers along the trace much to their liking, and after several months of such activity had amassed a fortune in gold and silver coins taken from unsuspecting migrants and businessmen. The Mason and Harpe gang were not content merely to rob their victims. The unfortunate travelers were often tortured, mutilated, murdered, and disemboweled, their dismembered parts stuffed into hollow trees or weighted down and sunk into nearby swamps. Unfortunately for Mason and Harpe, this activity attracted the attention of law enforcement officials.

While camping at a favorite rendezvous near Rocky Springs, located about forty miles northwest of Natchez, Mason suggested that the weight and size of their wealth was far too great for them to be carrying around. Up until then, the two men had transported their takings on the backs of two mules. The heavily burdened animals often slowed the outlaws down, a dangerous hindrance when they were fleeing from their pursuers. The two men decided to bury their gold and silver at the edge of their Rocky Springs camp site, and return to it as the need for funds arose. Shortly after concealing their fortune, they were chased by a group of vigilantes recently organized at Natchez. Mason and Harpe escaped, but their treasure remained hidden at Rocky Springs. According to investigators, it was never recovered.

In 1804, Harpe learned that there was a 2,000 dollar reward for his partner Mason, dead or alive. Seeing an opportunity to earn some easy money, the unscrupulous Harpe killed Mason, beheaded him, and carried the severed head to Greenfield, Mississippi, where he intended to claim the reward. On riding into the town, however, Harpe was immediately recognized and arrested. He was subsequently tried for his crimes and hanged.

The most famous desperado to terrorize the Natchez Trace was John Murrell. During his colorful outlaw career, Murrell made huge fortunes stealing and selling slaves, counterfeiting, and robbing travelers along the Natchez Trace. Because Murrell trusted no one, not even the members of his own gang, he secretly cached what researchers estimate to be hundreds of thousands of dollars' worth of gold and silver in coins, ingots, and nuggets at various locations along the famous route.

According to legend, Murrell hid several thousand dollars' worth of gold at the Devil's Punch Bowl, a large opening in a bluff just north of Natchez. Another location presumed to harbor some of Murrell's fortune is the site of an old cabin near the small settlement of Redwood. Murrell used the cabin for several months as a hideout, and once claimed to have buried a large portion of his treasure in the center of the dirt floor.

In 1834, Murrell was captured, tried, and sentenced to ten years of hard labor in the prison at Nashville, Tennessee. Murrell did not take well to confinement—he developed a severe case of tuberculosis and grew senile, and by the time he was released he was regarded as completely insane. When asked about the locations of the various treasures he had buried following his many robberies along the Natchez Trace, the old outlaw could remember nothing. Within weeks Murrell simply disappeared and was never seen again.

One of the most curious outlaws to frequent the Natchez Trace was Joseph T. Hare. Originally from Pennsylvania, Hare left home as a young lad and went to New York City where he found work as a tailor's apprentice. In this position, Hare developed a fondness for fine clothes, which distinguished him for the rest of his life.

Growing weary of cutting and stitching after several months, Hare found work on a ship, sailed up and down the east coast of North America for two years, and evenutally landed in New Orleans, a city that held great fascination for him. It was during this time that Hare discovered it was easier to rob hapless drunks than to hold down an honest job. He soon graduated to picking the pockets of the rich and prominent, and in a short time accumulated a handsome fortune, much of which he spent on fashionably tailored clothes for himself. By day he looked and acted the part of a dandy, but at night he was a merciless robber, often clubbing and killing his victims.

It was during his New Orleans experience that Hare learned of the impressive amount of traffic and trade that moved up and down the Natchez Trace. Stories of payrolls, merchandise, gold, silver, and mail fired the passions for even greater wealth that burned deep within Hare's breast. Perceiving the trace as a challenge as well as another step in his quest to become the richest man in the South, Hare enlisted three proficient robbers, armed and mounted all of them in fine style, and headed for the trace.

Hare was not a typical highwayman. For one thing, he maintained a diary in which he carefully recorded the amounts taken in each robbery, what the loot consisted of, and often even the names of those he had robbed. According to Hare's diary, he accumulated hundreds of thousands of dollars during the time he and his gang preyed on travelers along the trace.

Another characteristic that distinguished Hare from the ordinary robber was his selective sense of compassion. The same man who clubbed and killed was known, on several occasions, to have returned money to a victim when he learned it was needed to purchase food and clothing for a family.

Hare was also a complete gentleman during his robberies. He greeted both male and female victims with exaggerated politeness, inquiring after their health, and generally carrying on a pleasant conversation with them as he stripped them of their money and valuables. He often paused long enough to recite poetry to them, and during the last few months of his life he read passages from the Bible to those he robbed.

Like other bandits who roamed the Natchez Trace, Hare was known to have buried much of his loot. It has been well documented that he once cached 70,000 dollars in gold and silver coins on the outskirts of Fayette, a small town on the trace a short distance northwest of Natchez. On other occasions, he cached his booty in a small cave located near a swamp just off the trail north of Natchez.

Lawmen throughout Mississippi were out in full force in search of Hare, making his robberies increasingly difficult. After several narrow escapes from pursuing posses, Hare and his companions decided to quit the region for elsewhere, until things cooled off. After spending several weeks in Florida they traveled to New Orleans, and a short time later returned to the Natchez Trace and resumed robbing unsuspecting travelers.

Hare's luck was about to run out, however, for while robbing several men who were driving a small herd of cattle down the trace toward Natchez, he was arrested and sentenced to five years in jail. Most of his time in prison was spent adding to his journal and studying the Bible.

When Hare was finally released from prison in 1818, he drifted to Maryland, where he robbed a mail wagon of 16,900 dollars. He was arrested within the week. Interestingly, Hare was apprehended in a tailor shop while being fitted for a new suit of clothes. Following a lengthy trial, the notorious robber was sentenced to hang, and on September 10, 1818, he was executed on the gallows in Baltimore.

In his diary, Hare recorded a great deal of information relating to several treasures he cached along the Natchez Trace, treasures to which he was unable to return. Unfortunately, his directions to the troves are vague, and searchers have had no success with them. At today's values, the combined worth of Hare's hidden treasures would be several million dollars.

By 1835, the U.S. Government had widened the Natchez Trace and patrolled it often enough to discourage much of the robbery and killing which had plagued it for so long. Many of the Indians who resided in the area had been removed to assigned lands in the West, and as vast portions of the South opened up for settlement, the trace grew in importance as it accommodated increasing numbers of farmers, businessmen, and others who sought opportunities in Mississippi and Tennessee.

As thousands walked, rode, or were otherwise transported along the trace, few realized that alongside the trail at various places, millions of dollars' worth of gold, silver, jewelry, and cash lay buried. Most of it is still there.

Lost Chest of Gold Coins of Choctaw County

Somewhere in Choctaw County, along one bank of Pigeon Roost Creek, lies a fortune in gold coins buried just below the surface.

The treasure has a curious and rather exciting history involving a famous pirate, slaves, a beautiful Indian maiden, and a strange map.

The coins were originally taken by the notorious pirate Jean Lafitte during a raid on a commercial Spanish brigantine around 1813. Following the plundering of the vessel, Lafitte returned to his New Orleans stronghold, placed the coins in a wooden chest, and stored them with other booty he had accumulated during the previous months of piracy and raiding.

Several weeks later Lafitte decided to reward one of his favorite crewmen, Juan Cabrera, so he presented him with a gift of the chest of coins. (While merciless to his enemies, Lafitte was often quite generous to his friends.) Though he valued Cabrera's years of service, Lafitte told him the business of piracy was becoming far too risky and dangerous and suggested he take the gold, vanish into the interior, raise a family, and live the peaceful life of a gentleman.

Cabrera accepted Lafitte's offer and decided to travel to Mississippi and purchase a plantation. While making arrangements to leave, the seaman enjoyed several days and nights in New Orleans, spending some of his newfound riches on fine wine and new clothes.

One evening Cabrera met a young and beautiful Indian girl with whom he immediately fell in love. The girl had been brought to New Orleans as a slave of one John David Bradley, a self-described entrepreneur and businessman. Learning of this, Cabrera went to Bradley and, using some of the gold given to him by Lafitte, purchased the girl.

Several days later Cabrera and the Indian girl were married. Because the two enjoyed life in New Orleans so much, they decided to remain for a year before moving on to Mississippi. During that year they lived well and partook of the many pleasures the Crescent City had to offer. They also had a son.

Cabrera and his wife's former owner visited together from time to time, often sharing a fine meal and expensive brandy. One evening while smoking cigars after dining at a posh hotel, Cabrera told Bradley the story of Lafitte's gift of the chest filled with gold coins. It was the biggest mistake Cabrera ever made, and it eventually led to his death.

Cabrera did not see much of Bradley after that, but the businessman was alert to the seaman's every movement, always trying to detect some sign that might lead him to the treasure.

Finally the time arrived to depart for Mississippi. Cabrera, his wife and son, and two black slaves left New Orleans for the long journey that was to take them to what is now Choctaw County.

The Cabrera party traveled to the Mississippi River, crossed to Natchez by ferry, and journeyed up the Natchez Trace toward Choctaw County. During the long and some-times arduous trip, Cabrera could not shake the feeling that they were being followed, but he was never able to detect anyone behind them on the trail. As a precaution, Cabrera removed the gold-filled chest from the wagon each night, dragged it into the woods at the edge of camp, and concealed it in the underbrush. Each morning the chest was returned to the wagon.

Finally the party arrived in Choctaw County and decided to set up camp for the night. The next morning Cabrera would travel to the small settlement of Mathiston, where he would arrange for the purchase of some land. He selected a campsite next to Pigeon Roost Creek, a gentle stream that offered clear, fresh water. While the slaves, Crawford and Hinkle, were gathering firewood, Cabrera decided to hide the chest of coins. As he was walking toward the wagon, however, the peace of the camp was disturbed by the sudden arrival of four horsemen. It was Bradley in the company of three cutthroats. Riding boldly up to Cabrera, the intruder curtly demanded the gold coins.

Cabrera, surprised, cursed Bradley and ordered him to leave. Words were exchanged, Cabrera pulled Bradley off his horse, and a fight ensued. The scuffle lasted only a few seconds and when it was over Cabrera lay dying on the ground, a knife protruding from his chest.

Crawford and Hinkle returned to the campsite as Cabrera and Bradley were fighting. Fearing for the safety of the wife and child, the two slaves quickly placed them in the wagon and drove away.

Bradley believed that Cabrera had already buried the coins somewhere near the camp and ordered his followers to ignore the wagon and search the immediate area. While the bandits looked for the wooden chest, Crawford and Hinkle halted the wagon several hundred yards away along the creek, unloaded the chest as well as a few boxes of goods, and buried them near the bank. The woman and child were hidden in a dense thicket while the two slaves stood guard.

After dark, Cabrera's wife decided she would walk back to the camp to see what had become of her husband. The slaves tried to dissuade her from doing so but she was adamant.

Bravely she strode into the camp, where she found Bradley and the three men playing cards around the campfire. At the edge of the clearing, illuminated by the dancing and flickering light of the campfire, lay her husband's body. Screaming, she attempted to run to the corpse, but she was roughly seized by Bradley who demanded the gold. When she refused to reveal the location, he cuffed her sharply across the head. In response, Cabrera's widow pulled a knife from beneath her skirt and plunged it into her own breast. She died instantly.

Ignorant of their mistress's fate but fearing the worst, Crawford and Hinkle took the Cabrera baby and fled to the nearest Choctaw Indian village to beg for help. At sunrise the next morning, a party of Choctaw rode into the campsite and ordered Bradley and his men to leave. Once they were gone, the two slaves buried the bodies. Before abandoning the site where the coins were buried, Crawford scratched a crude map of the location on a piece of leather he found and placed it among some other goods in the back of the wagon.

Bradley retreated to New Orleans for awhile, but several years later returned to Mississippi and established a farm somewhere in the northern part of the state. Crawford and Hinkle took the baby and the wagon containing what remained of Cabrera's belongings and went to live with the Choctaw Indians.

The Choctaw, it was soon learned by the two slaves, were very superstitious about keeping the belongings of the dead, so they took the wagon out to a nearby meadow, dismantled it, and buried it along with all of its contents.

Crawford and Hinkle eventually married into the Indian tribe, and the Cabrera baby was taken in by a childless couple. As the boy grew to adulthood, he distinguished himself as a hunter and tracker, and at one point held some position of power among the Choctaw. Local legend claims that the boy, learning of the murder of his father by Bradley, hunted him down and killed him.

Sometime around 1921, a sharecropper named Crawford, a descendant of Cabrera's slave, was plowing a plot of ground not far from Pigeon Roost Creek near the old abandoned Choctaw campground. His plow became caught on something just below the surface, and when he investigated he found several pieces of an old wagon. Curious, he dug deeper and discovered several wooden boxes filled with household goods, tools, and some clothing. He also found a small clay pot filled with a few gold Spanish coins, as well as a strange map inscribed on a piece of leather.

Crawford was unaware of the significance of his find, having no knowledge whatsoever of the murder of the Cabrera family, the caching of the gold coins, or the involvement of his ancestor.

Several weeks later Crawford showed some of the coins to the owner of the land, a man named Mathis. When Mathis demanded to be taken to the site of the discovery, Crawford explained that the area had been plowed up and planted over. A violent argument ensued, Mathis threatened to kill Crawford, and the sharecropper stabbed the landowner and killed him. Crawford was later captured, tied to a tree, and burned to death.

Crawford's belongings fell into the hands of his son. While the younger Crawford did not fully understand the significance of the leather map, he was aware that it had something to do with the handful of gold Spanish coins found by his father.

Young Crawford entered the U.S. Army during World War II. Having seen action in Europe and distinguished himself in battle, he decided to make a career of the military. Though he traveled far and wide on various military assignments around the world, Crawford never forgot the strange leather map and vowed to someday return to Mississippi and attempt to decipher it.

During the Korean War Crawford was sent to Asia, where he was killed in action. His belongings, including the leather map, were given to his mother. Though she had no idea what the symbols on the map represented, she kept it among her son's possessions.

One day in the late 1950s, the elderly widow Crawford received a visitor. The man told her he had served in the army with her son and had learned of the existence of the leather map from him. Having some knowledge of the story of the Cabrera treasure buried somewhere along Pigeon Roost Creek, the stranger believed that the map would point to the location of the cache. He asked the widow Crawford if he could see it.

Mrs. Crawford was quite superstitious about such things and refused to show the map to anyone. Several times the man called on her and each time she sent him away. Finally tiring of the situation, the widow threw the map into her wood stove, vowing to be rid of the problem once and for all.

Much of the land near Pigeon Roost Creek had been converted to farmland during the early and middle parts of this century, but quite a bit of it was later abandoned and has since reverted to natural vegetation. In the region of the old Choctaw campground, pine trees and dense undergrowth have flourished and changed the appearance of the landscape.

Not far from the old Indian encampment and some-where near the bank of Pigeon Roost Creek lies a wooden chest filled with gold Spanish coins—unrecovered pirate loot whose legacy of death spanned several generations.

NORTH CAROLINA

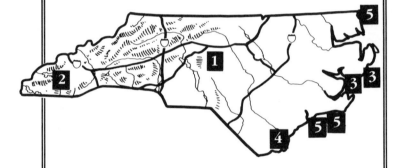

1. The Lost Clapham Silver Mine
2. Chief Sontechee's Silver Hoard
3. Blackbeard's Treasures
4. Coastal Treasure Cache of Stede Bonnet
5. Lost Spanish Treasure on the Outer Banks

The Lost Clapham
Silver Mine

Thomas Clapham traveled to the remote, mountainous country of North Carolina from his native Pennsylvania to seek his fortune by mining for precious metals. There, in the intrusive outcrops along the flanks of the Appalachian Mountains, Clapham discovered silver, grew wealthy, and eventually returned to his Pennsylvania home after concealing his rich mine. Treasure hunters have searched for the elusive lode ever since.

Thomas Clapham, accompanied by a black slave, had walked the many miles from his home in western Pennsylvania to what is now Randolph County, North Carolina. The year was 1765. Clapham had heard stories of discoveries of rich deposits of gold and silver in the hills and mountains far to the south. Warnings of hostile Indians, rugged wilderness, and outlaws did not deter the young Clapham, who believed it was his destiny to make his fortune as a miner.

Clapham and his slave spent several weeks wandering around the North Carolina Appalachians, searching for some sign of precious metals. Their meanderings finally brought them to an elevation called Horse Mountain. At the foot of the mountain, near a small spring, the two men set up a crude base camp in a shallow rock overhang. After putting in a decent supply of firewood, the two set out each morning to look for evidence of gold and silver on or near the mountain.

Weeks passed, and Clapham was growing more and more disappointed at his failure to locate a promising lode. In addition, the little spring near their camp had dried up. While searching for a new and dependable source of water, Clapham chanced to discover another spring on the west side of the mountain in a small canyon. Firewood was abundant and game was plentiful, so Clapham decided to change the location of his camp, believing the move would also change his luck. Clapham followed the small stream that emanated from the spring down a gentle slope, and discovered it entered a creek some seventy yards away. This stream is known today as Richland Creek. The next morning, the two men moved to the new site.

While clearing debris from the spring, Clapham made a discovery that was to change his life. As he was raking away several years' accumulation of leaves, branches, and dirt from the mouth of the spring, he detected some color in the shallow water. Plunging his hands into the cool, clear pool next to the opening in the rock, he pulled out two large silver nuggets. Excited, Clapham searched the bottom of the narrow stream for several feet, eventually collecting a handful of silver nuggets.

Encouraged by his find, Clapham ordered his slave to begin construction of a log cabin. He was determined to live comfortably through the approaching winter while he continued his search for ore in the area.

As the slave worked on the cabin and hunted for game, Clapham searched for the source of the silver. After several weeks, he located it in a bare granite exposure, about forty feet uphill from the water source. All through the winter and the following spring, Clapham and the slave dug almost pure silver from a thick vein, eventually excavating a narrow shaft that penetrated nearly two dozen feet into the side of the canyon wall.

When spring arrived and the winter snow finally melted, Clapham was visited by a large party of Cherokee Indians. Though he had heard many stories of hostile Indians in the region, Clapham had seen none until now.

The Indians appeared angry and, using sign language, ordered Clapham to leave the area. Clapham maintained a friendly demeanor and presented the Indians with gifts of tobacco and a few extra blankets he had brought with him for just such an emergency. As Clapham and several of the tribe's elders sat in a circle conversing in signs, a few of the braves wandered about the area, examining the canyon. Clapham feared they would discover his mining activities on the side of the canyon wall and kill him.

A few of the Indians found the spring and drank water from it, others explored up and down the small narrow canyon, but none of them noticed the shaft on the hillside.

After about two hours, the Indians departed. While their demeanor was still somewhat threatening, they no longer demanded that Clapham leave the area.

Clapham, however, remained concerned about the presence of the angry Indians, and from that point on he and his slave worked in the mine only at night. Because his accumulation of silver nuggets was growing large, Clapham decided to construct a small smelter in which to melt down his silver and fashion it into ingots. Locating a suitable site nearly a mile from his cabin, he built a crude furnace. The site was far from any trails the Cherokee might travel and sufficiently out of sight to escape detection by the casual hunter or trapper.

In time, Clapham accumulated enough silver ingots to fully load all of his pack animals. Realizing he possessed a fortune, he decided to quit the area and return to Pennsylvania.

Clapham destroyed the smelter and removed or covered all traces of it. Next, he and the slave filled in the mine and covered the entrance with large boulders, making it look like any other section of the canyon wall.

At the mouth of the canyon, Clapham inscribed cryptic directions to his mine on a large granite boulder, and then made several slashes on nearby trees.

While packing and loading his belongings, Clapham discovered a small sack filled with silver nuggets which he had forgotten to melt down. Placing the nuggets in a copper cooking pot, he carried them to nearby Richland Creek and buried them at the base of a large poplar tree on which he made another long slash.

The next day, as Clapham and the slave were riding out of the area, they chanced upon another settler who lived about ten miles from Clapham's cabin. The settler, a man named Peter Elliot, invited the two travelers to stay for dinner.

During the meal, Clapham told Elliot about his silver mine and showed him the packs filled with silver ingots. He also talked about burying the cooking pot filled with silver nuggets. Clapham was vague about directions to the mine, and told Elliot he intended to return someday and file a claim on the land.

The next day, Clapham and the slave rode away, never to return. During the next few years, Elliot searched for the mine and the potful of silver nuggets, but was unable to find either of them.

Sometime during the 1840s, a descendant of Thomas Clapham found an old trunk containing personal effects and papers belonging to the miner. Among the papers was a journal which revealed the existence of the rich silver mine in Randolph County. Along with the chronology of events, there were descriptions of the region, the location of the mine, and the caching of the silver nuggets in the copper cooking pot. The descendant, excited by the possibility of instant wealth waiting in the North Carolina Appalachians, decided to make a trip to the area and file a claim. Though he searched for several weeks, he was never able to locate the small canyon described by Thomas Clapham.

In the 1960s, a man named W.C. Hammond operated a small farm near Horse Mountain in Randolph County. One day, two men appeared at his farm and requested permission to search for treasure on his property. The men showed Hammond a book containing directions to the Clapham silver mine, and claimed they were financed by a Clapham heir.

One page of the book described the large rock on which Thomas Clapham had scratched directions. The inscription reportedly read, "150 feet east, then back nine feet towards A.M.I."

Hammond had heard stories of lost silver mines in this area many times before, but had never believed them. He granted permission to the two men to search the area, but told them they would likely find nothing. During the next few days, Hammond observed the activities of the men, and was not surprised to see them depart without finding the mine.

Around 1968, the rock bearing Clapham's inscription was found by a man named Henderson Barrow. The rock was described as a dense granite boulder, recently fractured as a result of severe frost. The entire inscription, however, was intact, with letters approximately two to three inches high and reading exactly as described in the journal seen earlier by Hammond. Barrow searched the area for several weeks, but was unable to locate the mine.

As a result of the interest generated by Barrow's discovery, several others entered the area around this time, attempting to locate the elusive mine. All were unsuccessful.

Sometime during the 1970s, a young man exchanged several silver nuggets for cash in nearby Greensboro. When asked where he obtained the nuggets, the man said he found them in an old copper pot on the bank of Richland Creek in Randolph County. He claimed the creek had eroded away part of the bank, exposing the pot and its contents.

After making the exchange, the young man left and was never seen again.

If the spot where the man found the copper pot filled with silver nuggets could be relocated, the lost silver mine of Thomas Clapham would not be far away. Somewhere near the Richland Creek bank would lie the small, narrow canyon from which the Pennsylvanian extracted a fortune in silver in 1765.

Chief Sontechee's
Silver Hoard

Many are the legends and tales of lost, hidden, and buried treasures in the North Carolina Appalachians, the Piedmont, and the coastal plain region. In the western part of the state Cherokee Indians, once a dominant tribe in the area, figure prominently in many of the stories. Chief Sontechee, the last member of a little-known branch of the Cherokee Indians, stood guard for many years over a hoard of silver that was likely worth millions of dollars. Following Sontechee's death, the cave where the silver was stored was covered by a landslide, and treasure hunters have been searching for it ever since.

Sontechee was a member of a band of Cherokee Indians which hunted, fished, and farmed a portion of the North Carolina Appalachians known as the Nantahala Mountains, near what is now the northern part of Macon County. Over many generations, these Indians mined silver from the mountains for use in making jewelry and ornaments. Fascinated by the dense, shiny metal, the Cherokee gathered great amounts of it at a time and stored it in a large cave near the mouth of Factory Creek, not far from their settlement.

The early white settlers in this area were not unfriendly toward the native Cherokee, but they inadvertantly brought with them diseases to which the Indians had little or no immunity. In time, many of the Cherokee died from these diseases, and numerous isolated branches of the tribe living in remote portions of the Appalachians were completely wiped out.

Sontechee's band was no exception. Sometime during the early 1800s, this group of Cherokee was stricken with smallpox, and all but Sontechee died. As soon as the Indians no longer dominated the land near the Little Tennessee River south of the Great Smoky Mountains, the whites moved into the region and took over many of the prosperous farms established by the Cherokee. Sontechee, driven from the old Indian settlement near what is now the town of Franklin, moved into the cave that held the tribe's store of silver.

Sontechee was tolerated by most of the white settlers, and many of them eventually grew friendly toward the harmless old Indian, often providing him with gifts of vegetables harvested from their gardens. In turn, Sontechee would bring them fish from nearby streams and perform chores on their farms. On occasion, the old Indian would present one or another of the white families with a gift of a silver nugget.

Many of the settlers were curious as to the source of Sontechee's silver, but the Indian never responded to questions about the ore.

Though Sontechee never held a formal office with his tribe, the whites referred to him as "chief." Chief Sontechee became a regular visitor to the growing settlement of Franklin, often paying for supplies with nuggets of almost pure silver.

On several occasions, some of the townsfolk attempted to follow Sontechee back to his cave, hoping to discover the source of his silver. Most people thought the Indian dug it from a nearby mine, and none remotely suspected that a huge accumulation of the precious ore was stored deep within the very cave in which the Indian lived.

Sontechee became close friends with a family that farmed the rich flood plain along a portion of the Little Tennessee River. The farmer appreciated Sontechee's visits—the Indian was a good worker who helped the farmer in many ways and he often spent time with his children, teaching them the ways of the forest animals and showing them how to track, hunt, and trap.

As Sontechee grew older and more infirm, he found the trip along the rocky, winding trail from his cave to the farm increasingly difficult. Noticing that the Indian was growing weaker and more tired with each passing day, the farmer invited him to live on the farm. Sontechee accepted the invitation, returning to his cave only rarely. When he did, he always returned with a gift of a large silver nugget for the farmer.

One evening, Sontechee called the farmer to his bedside. The Indian told him he did not expect to live long enough to see the sun rise the next morning, and wanted the farmer to know the location of the rich store of Cherokee silver. He told the farmer of the many packs of silver nuggets that had been dug from the granite outcrops in the hills to the north and carried back to the encampment near the Nantahala Mountains. He told him of the leather containers filled with almost pure silver, stacked high in the back of the cave in which he had lived alone for so many years. Before he died, Sontechee gave the farmer directions to the cave and told him to retrieve all of the silver stored there and put it to good use among his people.

After burying Sontechee the next morning, the farmer set off to locate the cave described by the old Indian. After about half a day of riding, he arrived at the location, only to discover that the entire region had been hit by a recent landslide which had covered the entrance to the cavern.

Though he climbed around the side of the mountain for the remainder of the day, the farmer was unable to find the location of the cave entrance.

Over the years, many have searched for the cave containing the treasure in silver. Many believed they had pinpointed the location, but were unable to remove the covering of rock and debris that has concealed it for well over a century.

Nearby, remains of an old smelter have been found, where it is believed that the Cherokee sometimes melted down the ore and poured it into molds. It is likely that, in addition to ore, ingots of almost pure silver may be stacked among the full packs of nuggets in Sontechee's lost cave. If so, the possibility exists that an incredible fortune lies in the cave, a fortune hidden only by the residue of a landslide, located somewhere in the southern foothills of the Nantahala Mountains.

Blackbeard's Treasures

Of all the notorious pirates who roamed, terrorized, and pillaged the Atlantic coast of North America, none is more famous than Blackbeard. After 250 years of debate, most scholars believe that Blackbeard's real name was Edwin Teach. It is also believed that he hid millions of dollars' worth of treasure at various locations along the coast of North Carolina.

Blackbeard was notable in many ways. His reign of terror along the Atlantic seaboard as he attacked merchant and trading vessels and fled with their cargo is legendary. In the process he killed many men and sank numerous ships.

His appearance was also noteworthy. A large and muscular man, he sported a grand, black, bushy beard which he combed and set with wax each morning. By nature hirsute, Teach's great beard almost merged with his head of thick, dark hair. Both hair and beard were often plaited into tails and decorated with colorful ribbons.

Blackbeard showed a preference for the coast of North Carolina as a place to retreat after long and arduous campaigns at sea. At one time he had three residences there—Edenton, Elizabeth City, and Okracoke, and it is rumored he had wives at each of these locations.

Though Teach was recognized as a ruthless pirate by all of the citizens along the coast, he was tolerated and even enthusiatically accepted by them because of the goods and money he brought into the area. During this time, North

Carolina was a very poor region, and the citizens desperately needed the supplies and the income provided by the pirate. Blackbeard offered much of his stolen goods to area merchants at incredibly cheap prices. The merchants, in turn, would sell the needed goods at a high profit. Everyone was happy, and even North Carolina's Governor Eden turned a blind eye to these illegal transactions.

The arrangement was not to last, however. Many of the higher-minded citizens living along the coast of North Carolina petitioned the governor to get rid of the murderous pirate and his crew. During this time, Blackbeard had the nerve to occasionally raid small and defenseless North Carolina settlements, incurring further wrath from the residents.

Where the governor of North Carolina was weak and tolerant of Teach, Alexander Spotswood, then governor of Virginia, decided that the larcenous and murderous activities of the famous freebooter must come to an end.

Having failed at procuring cooperation from Governor Eden, Spotswood took it upon himself to arm and commission several warships in secret, and ordered a competent Navy captain, Robert Maynard, to lead a punitive expedition to the Carolina coast and do away with the notorious pirate once and for all.

A scout ship located Teach and his pirate fleet, which was anchored at Okracoke Inlet, in November of 1718. Blackbeard had observed the scout ship, but could not believe anyone would be foolish enough to attack him and his fearsome crew. On the morning of November 22, however, warships under the leadership of Maynard sailed into the inlet and attacked the unprepared pirates. Before he met his death, Edwin Teach suffered twenty-five sword wounds and five gunshot wounds. When Blackbeard went down for the last time, the remaining pirates, now without a leader, either surrendered or escaped to shore.

Teach's head was severed from his body and hung from the bowsprit. Upon order from Spotswood, the severed head was delivered to him in Virginia.

Once the menace of Blackbeard had been eliminated from the region, many citizens, aware of stories of buried treasures near the dead pirate's haunts, began to search in earnest for hidden riches. Many were the tales of buried gold and silver coins, of cached jewels, and of bars of gold hidden along deserted shores.

One famous tale of a Blackbeard treasure involves a heavy brick and timber vault, which was allegedly dumped into the Pamlico Inlet prior to an attack on Teach's pirate fleet. Teach had ordered the construction of a large vault in which to store his gold coins. The vault was lashed to the ship's deck, and filled with the riches. During the attack, Blackbeard was determined that his treasure not fall into the hands of his pursuers, so he ordered it dumped overboard into shallow water.

Sometime during the 1930s, two men were fishing in the inlet, not far from the present-day town of Washington. While casting for game fish from a small boat, the lines of one of the fishermen became entangled in something below the surface. On investigation, it was discovered that the fishhook was lodged in an exposed timber near the bottom—a timber which had been part of the roof of Teach's treasure vault. Breaking through the rotted roof, the men discovered three large cooking pots, each filled to the top with gold coins. With great effort, the two fishermen spent the remainder of the day removing the gold from its shallow burial place and caching it on the nearby shore.

After examining the coins, the fishermen noted that they had all been minted in 1700, lending further credence to the belief that they were part of Blackbeard's hoard. The two decided they needed to do some serious thinking about the disposition of the gold coins, and for the meantime they decided to bury them in a nearby cypress grove and return for them later.

For nearly a year, the two fishermen made elaborate plans to retrieve and invest the treasure. Unfortunately, one of them was stricken with a fever and died. The second man decided to dig up the treasure and keep it all for himself.

Returning to the area where the gold had been buried nearly a year earlier, the man was shocked to discover that the landscape had undergone significant changes. Heavy rains earlier in the year had swollen the Pamlico River, causing great flood waters to rush down the channel and into the inlet. In the process, the river had changed course and uprooted and carried away hundreds of trees growing along its banks, including the entire cypress grove where the coins had been buried. Though he searched for several days, the distraught fisherman could not relocate the treasure site.

Another Blackbeard treasure is associated with a large tree on Okracoke Island. Teach allegedly buried a big wooden chest filled with gold and silver coins at the base of this tree in 1717. He made several cryptic slashes on the trunk with his sword, and thereafter referred to it as the Money Tree.

The legend of the Money Tree endured over the succeeding centuries, and sometime during the 1950s, two men who were familiar with the tale believed they had finally located the tree. It had a huge base, was obviously quite old, and grew on a portion of Okracoke Island known to have been frequented by the noted pirate. Furthermore, there were several marks on the trunk that suggested it had been deeply cut many years earlier. An initial scanning with a metal detector of an area next to the tree indicated a large deposit of something metallic just below the surface.

The two men returned the next day with picks and shovels, intending to retrieve what they believed to be one of Blackbeard's great fortunes. They enlisted the help of a local fisherman and his son. Together the four of them proceeded to dig, but they encountered an incredible tangle of thick roots within the first two feet. The roots were so dense, twisted, and matted that further digging was impossible.

The men decided at that point to rent or borrow some heavy equipment to facilitate their task. The fisherman, an elderly man, reminded the others that the tree was on private property and that the owner of the land should be consulted prior to bringing machinery into the area. All agreed, and they went to the visit the owner, whose housekeeper informed them that he would be away for two weeks.

Family illness kept the landowner out of state for several months, but upon his return he was visited by the two treasure hunters. They described their discovery, explained their intentions, and were relieved and pleased to find him intrigued by the prospect of a fortune located on his property. The three of them agreed to divide the chest of gold and silver they believed lay among the twisted roots of the large tree.

Together they drove to the tree to examine it. They soon discovered, however, that the great tree had been toppled and dragged several yards from its original location. A heavy drag line attached to the trunk suggested that someone had used heavy equipment to pull it from its growth site.

Suspecting the fisherman, the two treasure hunters and the landowner traveled to his home, only to learn it had been sold. It was explained to them that the old fisherman had recently come into some money and moved to a nice new home in another city!

One legend that is current along the coast of North Carolina involves Blackbeard's ghost. A shimmering, headless form is often seen moving slowly along some lonely shore, carrying a lantern. Those familiar with the legend claim that the ghost is searching for its head. For several hours, the ghost can be observed wandering the beaches of Okracoke Island as well as other places nearby. Eventually, the ghost places the lantern on the ground, and it is believed that this marks the site of some long-buried treasure. But once the lantern is set down, the light and the form last for only a few seconds longer, then vanish into the night mist, once again confusing those still hopeful of finding Blackbeard's lost treasures.

Coastal Treasure Cache of Stede Bonnet

The North Carolina coast was a favorite haunt of eighteenth century pirates, and as a result of the frequency of their visits to these shores many legends and tales of lost and buried treasures have originated in this region.

One of the more interesting pirates to frequent the waters off the North Carolina coast was Stede Bonnet. Bonnet's background was remarkably different from that of most of the noted buccaneers of the day—he came from a well-to-do family, had attended the finest schools and academies, and was a retired British army officer.

In 1717 Bonnet was living with his wife and child on the island of Barbados, located at the extreme eastern end of the Caribbean Sea. Bonnet owned a large plantation and raised blooded horses. His days were spent riding across his extensive landholdings and directing the field hands, while his evenings were filled with the sipping of fine brandy in the dining rooms of the best hotels in Bridgetown, the capital.

For reasons that are unclear, Bonnet decided to abandon the security and good life he had found on Barbados and dedicate himself to piracy. One story claims he did so to escape his wife, whom he apparently hated with a passion. Others say he simply was bored with the role of gentleman farmer and craved adventure. In any case, he purchased a ship at Bridgetown, rounded up a crew of from thirty to forty cutthroats and ne'er-do-wells from the local taverns and docks, and set a course for Virginia.

Though a skilled military tactician while serving in the British army, Bonnet proved to be quite inept on the open sea. He possessed no skills important to a seaman, had very little sense of direction, and was generally regarded by his crew as unfit to command a vessel. He did have the good sense, however, to appoint a competent first mate and other officers.

In spite of his lack of nautical aptitude, Bonnet became very successful as a pirate and quickly gained a reputation for his ruthlessness. On the way to Virginia his ship, which he named the *Revenge,* overtook three merchant vessels. He plundered them, and then set them afire after forcing the crews into lifeboats and leaving them to the mercy of the sea.

Impressed with his early successes, Bonnet decided to sail up and down the Atlantic Coast from New England to the waters of the Carolinas, preying on cargo ships and occasionally raiding small settlements. In a short time Bonnet collected a large amount of gold and silver which he stored in several wooden chests in the ship's cabin.

For a short time, Bonnet teamed up with the notorious Edwin Teach, better known as Blackbeard. The two of them plundered and raided along the coast, and it was Teach who introduced Bonnet to the many pleasant stretches along the North Carolina shore. Following a successful raid, Bonnet would often retreat to this area where he would refurbish his ships and provide his crew time to rest before the next major expedition.

As Bonnet grew increasingly successful as a pirate, he began to attract the attention of the British authorities, who in turn launched several warships in pursuit of the freebooter.

In response, Bonnet changed the name of his ship from the *Revenge* to the *Royal James.* He also changed his own name to James Thomas, assuming that if he encountered a British pursuit ship his new identity would fool them. During this time he appropriated a second vessel and added it to his raiding party.

Under his new name, Bonnet continued to sail up and down the coast attacking merchant ships and in time added two more ships to his small pirate fleet. After a series of successful raids, the Royal James as well as the three other ships were so burdened with captured gold, silver, and goods that Bonnet decided it was necessary to put to port and store much of the take. In addition, recent encounters had severely battered his small fleet to the point that repairs needed to be made.

To this end, Bonnet ordered his ships into the Cape Fear Inlet near the extreme southeastern coast of North Carolina, close to the site of the present-day town of Wilmington. After assessing the damage to the ships, he determined that several planks and timbers needed to be replaced in order to restore the vessels to seaworthy condition. Having neither the time nor the desire to venture into the forest to cut trees and fashion and cure the beams and planks, Bonnet simply ordered his crew to capture a ship and strip the needed materials from it.

This decision proved to be a grave mistake for the pirate. The local fishermen who lived along the inlet were incensed at the theft and destruction of one of their boats and decided to report the pirates to the authorities. One William Rhett of Charles Town (now Charleston, South Carolina), about 150 miles to the south, petitioned the governor to establish and arm an expedition to arrest and punish the malefactors. As Bonnet and his crew worked on the ships and rested on the Carolina coast, a well-organized force of sailors and citizens was closing in on Cape Fear Inlet in two heavily-armed vessels, the *Henry* and the *Sea Nymph.*

Bonnet knew nothing of the expedition sent to capture him until the two ships sailed into the inlet. Stationing the two vessels in positions to block any escape attempt, the pursuers, unsure of how well-armed the pirate ships were, decided to wait and see what Bonnet would do.

During the second night of this standoff, Bonnet decided at least two of his ships were seaworthy enough to attack the *Henry* and the *Sea Nymph*. Realizing there was a chance they might be defeated, Bonnet ordered three large wooden chests filled with gold coins loaded into one of the rowboats. The coins represented a portion of the treasure taken from various merchant ships during the past year, and amounted to a huge fortune.

Accompanied only by his two most trusted crewmen, Bonnet rowed to the nearest shore, dragged the chests several yards up the beach, and buried them.

The next morning, Bonnet steered two ships toward the *Henry* and the *Sea Nymph*. When the vessels were within cannon range, firing commenced and a vicious battle ensued. For half a day the ships reeled under the heavy cannon fire, all of them suffering severe damage. Finally the *Royal James,* which had taken the worst beating, began to take on water. As the boat sank to the bottom of the inlet, Bonnet, along with the crew members, was hauled out of the water and placed in chains. That same afternoon, the *Henry* and the *Sea Nymph* limped southward along the coast to Charles Town, where they delivered their prisoners.

The crew members were all executed within two days. When the authorities learned they had finally captured the elusive Stede Bonnet, they retained him in a cell for a period of three weeks, questioning him about his pirate acivities during the previous year. Free to leave his cell to exercise from time to time, Bonnet escaped at one point but was quickly recaptured and returned to his chains.

Another three weeks passed and Bonnet, heavily manacled and chained, was led to the gallows. As the noose was tied around his neck, someone placed a bouquet of flowers in his hands. Seconds later the trap door was released and Bonnet's limp form was swinging beneath the wooden floor of the gallows, the flowers dropping to the ground one by one.

For years people believed that Bonnet's treasure went to the bottom of Cape Fear Inlet along with the *Royal James*. The existence of the great treasure in gold coins cached somewhere on the beach was revealed one day, however, by an old seaman who had had too much to drink at a dockside tavern in the port of Georgetown, located on the South Carolina coast between Wilmington and Charleston.

The seaman claimed that he was one of the crewmen who had helped Bonnet bury his treasure that dark night prior to the battle. The next morning, as the *Royal James* sank, the seaman had managed to avoid capture by hiding behind some floating debris. He eventually reached shore and fled from the area. While he wished to return and retrieve Bonnet's treasure, he feared he would be recognized, captured, and executed. He decided to wait a few years and then venture back to the secret location on the inlet and dig up the gold coins.

Several men were seated around the old seaman's table listening to his tale. One or two mocked him, not believing a word of the story. Two others grew very interested and pressed the old man for details. Plying him with drinks, they attempted to get the old pirate to reveal the location of the buried chests. When he refused, the two men grew angry.

Finally it was time for the old man to retire to his room. As he staggered from the tavern and into the dark streets, he was followed by the two whose greed had been stirred by his tale of buried treasure. Out of reach of the lights from the tavern, they jumped the old man and threatened to kill him if he did not reveal the location of the gold coins. The pirate refused to comply and they slit his throat, nearly decapitating him. They tossed his body into a nearby salt marsh where it was not found for several days.

Bonnet's treasure chests filled with gold coins still lie beneath the sandy beach somewhere on the Cape Fear Inlet. This incredible fortune has eluded searchers for over two and a half centuries but still they come to Cape Fear, each believing he will be the one to uncover Bonnet's fabulous cache.

Lost Spanish Treasure on the Outer Banks

It was the middle of August, 1750, and the four heavily laden Spanish ships were undertaking the long voyage from the Caribbean Sea across the Atlantic Ocean to Spain. Each of the vessels was carrying tax receipts from the previous five years, all of which had been converted into gold and silver. The ships, under the command of General Juan Manuel de Bonilla, had picked up chests of coins and loads of ingots at several ports along the coast of Mexico, and at several Caribbean islands. Bonilla and his crew were under orders to carry the tax revenues to the port of Valencia on the Mediterranean Sea, where they would be transferred to a pack train consisting of more than a hundred donkeys and transported to the treasury at Madrid, the capital.

The fleet was composed of the *Nuestra Señora de Guadalupe,* the *Nuestra Señora de Soledad,* the *El Salvador,* and the *La Casca.* All four ships had proven seaworthy during previous voyages and the crew was composed of experienced seamen. Bonilla, a skillful navigator and leader of men, had crossed the Atlantic Ocean several times.

For several years, the Spanish government had delayed the transportation of collected taxes across the Atlantic Ocean because of the ongoing War of the Austrian Succession. Enemy ships patrolled the coast of the Iberian Peninsula and often attacked Spanish vessels, confiscating the cargoes and killing the crews. As a result of the long delay, the accumulation of gold and silver was impressive, and researchers suggest it was worth several million dollars. When the war ended, seagoing traffic across the Atlantic Ocean resumed.

The most efficient way to sail from the New World to Spain was along the east coast of North America on the Gulf Stream to a point near Virginia, and then eastward across the Atlantic and through the Strait of Gibraltar.

As the Spanish fleet sailed northeastward several miles off the South Carolina coast, the skies began to darken and the winds picked up. Unkown to Bonilla, a great hurricane was developing several miles out in the Atlantic to the southeast. Believing he might be able to outrun the storm, Bonilla decided not to seek shelter among the many bays and inlets available along this part of the coast. He continued onward, a decision that proved to be fatal.

By the time the fleet reached a point opposite Wilmington in what is now North Carolina, the storm had become so severe that the high winds were tearing sails and toppling masts, and the violent waves were buffeting the light ships like so much kindling in the raging sea. Realizing that to remain on the open ocean was to court death, Bonilla directed the fleet into Okracoke Inlet and anchored the ships in the relatively calm waters of Pamlico Sound. Somewhat protected by a long barrier island, the sailors waited out the storm in relative safety.

Separating Pamlico Sound and the Atlantic Ocean are a series of elongated barrier islands composed of sand, stretching from several miles to the south near present-day Morehead City, South Carolina, and northward to Virginia. These barrier islands are called the Outer Banks, and were nicknamed the "Graveyard of the Atlantic" by early sailors. It is estimated that hundreds of ships have been sunk by storms in this region.

Once the hurricane abated, Bonilla ordered an inspection of the vessels. All had suffered some damage but were deemed seaworthy, save for the *Nuestra Señora de Guadalupe.*

The *Guadalupe,* which was armed with seventy-five cannons, was severely damaged and barely able to remain afloat. While crewmen worked desperately to save the vessel, others unloaded the precious cargo of gold and silver and placed it in the holds of the other three ships. A large portion of the treasure carried by the *Guadalupe* had been transferred to the other boats when the ship finally took on too much water and sank to the bottom of the sound, carrying several chests of gold and silver with it.

Bonilla, unequipped to salvage the sunken treasure and in a hurry to deliver the taxes to Spain, ordered the ships back out through Okracoke Inlet and onto the open ocean. Once at sea, however, the fleet was struck almost immediately by another severe storm.

The captain of the *Nuestra Señora de Soledad* either lost his bearings or was blown off course, for the vessel veered southwestward and was soon lost from view.

Legend relates that the *Soledad* was blown toward the shore near Atlantic Beach close to present-day Morehead City. Before reaching the shore, however, it broke apart and sank, carrying well over a million dollars' worth of gold and silver to the sandy bottom. None of the crew survived.

The *El Salvador,* also blown southwestward by the strong winds, was trying make a landing near Cape Lookout, not far from Atlantic Beach, when she began to break up. Despite the raging storm, several crewmen managed to leave the ship and swim to shore. The *El Salvador* was also carrying a heavy cargo of gold and silver, all of which went to the bottom along with her.

The last ship to leave Pamlico Sound, the *La Casca,* continued northeastward for a while, but was eventually blown toward shore near the North Carolina-Virginia border. The ship, its sails tattered and useless, was completely out of control when it smashed aground at Currituck Inlet. The wooden vessel broke apart and its rich cargo was scattered for dozens of yards along the shore. Very little of the treasure transported by the *La Casca* was recovered, and it is believed that residents of the area gathered it up after the storm subsided.

When the Spanish government learned of the disaster that had struck the treasure fleet, it quickly ordered a recovery ship to the region to reclaim as much of the gold and silver as possible. This vessel, however, was unable to locate the wreckage of any of the ships save for the *La Casca,* but by then it was too late to retrieve any of the cargo.

Of the other three ships that went down, only the *El Salvador* has been located to date. A salvager who had searched for many years for the sunken vessel near Cape Lookout finally located it and removed several bars of silver from the wrecked hull lying half-buried in the bottom sands. Efforts continue to locate and retrieve more of the valuable cargo.

The Spanish treasure fleet of 1750 represents only a few of the ships that have gone down near the Outer Banks. There are maps and journals available which indicate that as many as 600 ships sank along the Outer Banks between 1585 and 1970. Many of these vessels, like the Spanish fleet of 1750, were undoubtedly carrying rich cargoes of gold, silver, currency, and jewelry. Some have been found and portions of their loads recovered, but most of them still lie below the surface of the ocean, their treasures covered by the ever-shifting sands of the ocean bottom.

South Carolina

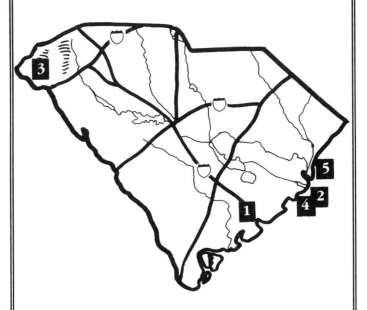

1. Lost Pirate Treasures in the South Carolina
   Tidal Marsh
2. Found: The Long-lost Treasure of the
   SS *Central America*
3. The Indian Gold Mine de Soto Never Found
4. Sunken Art Treasures in the Atlantic
5. Bullion and Arms Off North Island

Lost Pirate Treasures in the South Carolina Tidal Marsh

The Atlantic coastal town of Charleston, South Carolina, is located on the shore of an inlet on a point of land between the Ashley and Cooper Rivers. Charles Towne, as it was named originally and known until 1783, was a growing community with thriving businesses, and its port received ships from afar bearing cargoes of rum, sugar, molasses, fruit, silk, and precious stones. These rich and varied cargoes were unloaded at the port of Charleston and brokered by local business entrepreneurs. Much of what arrived here was purchased by local residents. The remainder was loaded onto wagons and transported into the interior, where it was sold in the new settlements that could be found in the foothills of the Appalachian Mountains.

To the west of Charleston lay a vast, swampy environment known as a tidal marsh. This low-lying, boggy setting was characterized by shallow, murky water interrupted here and there by small islands of silt and clusters of dense vegetation. These marshes were generally avoided by most people because they were thickly infested with poisonous snakes and hordes of mosquitoes. Quicksand was an ever-present hazard, as was the likelihood of becoming lost in the mazes of islands and complex aquatic passageways.

A few individuals, however, found the tidal marsh to their liking, and took advantage of the forbidden nature of this primitive-looking habitat to conceal millions of dollars' worth of gold, silver, jewels, and other treasures. From all accounts, most of the treasures hidden in the tidal marsh near Charleston are still there.

The first record of anyone using the tidal marsh to conceal treasure concerns a man who was likely the best-known and most notorious pirate ever to ply the waters of the Atlantic Coast and the Caribbean Sea. Popularly known as Blackbeard, this brigand was born in England to a family named Drummond. As he grew older, young Drummond joined the British navy, enlisting, for reasons still unknown, under the name of Edwin Teach. While serving with the British navy, Drummond, a k a Teach, was an able and competent student, learning the art and craft of sailing so well that he became something of an expert.

Drummond's lust for adventure, however, far exceeded any opportunities provided him by the British navy. He eventually mustered out, obtained his own vessel, and began a career of piracy along the Atlantic Coast and in the West Indies. Blackbeard's travels occasionally took him to the windward island of Barbados where he became aligned with many others of his ilk, and before long he found himself in command of an entire fleet of pirate ships which preyed upon commercial vessels sailing the waters between Europe and the New World, vessels that carried fortunes in precious metals and other goods.

Blackbeard was a theatrical agent's dream. His thick, black, heavy beard practically covered the upper part of his chest, and he would sometimes tie ribbons of many different colors into it, letting their long ends stream behind him. Around his waist he wrapped colorful sashes into which he stuck pistols, knives, and cutlasses.

As a pirate, Blackbeard was fearless, ruthless, and gave quarter to no one. He was known to kill men, women, and children alike. He never shied from battle, and usually led the attack on any ship his cutthroats overtook and boarded.

Throughout his many years of terrorizing the Atlantic seas, Blackbeard amassed an incredible fortune in gold and silver bullion and coins, as well as a king's ransom in jewels. Following several successful plunders, Blackbeard always fled with his booty to the still waters of Charleston harbor.

During his journeys up and down the coast of North America, Blackbeard had visited the port of Charleston many times, and eventually fell in love with the locale. He enjoyed the waterfront environment, where he could be found carousing with several women at a time and drinking with other pirates who frequented the area. Blackbeard loved the peace and serenity of Charleston, and purchased a large, well-furnished house and several acres of land there. Blackbeard was also enamored of Charleston for a more pragmatic reason—he was attracted to the nearby tidal marsh as a nearly impenetrable place in which to conceal the many treasures he had accumulated. Sealing his coins, bullion, and jewely into wooden casks, Blackbeard himself would load several at a time onto a skiff and singlehandedly row out into the marsh and hide them in some preselected location. It is estimated that, given today's value of such items, several millions of dollars' worth of the famous pirate's treasure was secreted in the swamp.

In 1670, the government offered a general pardon to all pirates and other marauders if they would simply turn themselves in and return all the items they had stolen. The offer of a pardon appealed to Blackbeard, who was tiring of the constant pursuit and harassment by authorities and believed it was only a matter of time before he was caught and executed. But the pirate did not want to give up his fabulous wealth, so well hidden in the tidal marsh. By bribing high government officials, Blackbeard obtained his pardon at a minimal cost and was able to keep his treasure as well.

Now that he was an extremely wealthy man no longer pursued by the authorities, Blackbeard married a sixteen-year-old girl and made plans to purchase a large plantation. His lust for adventure on the high seas was not easily quelled, however, and only a few months later the colorful freebooter reassembled his band of cutthroats and once again took to a life of piracy on the high seas.

This time, Blackbeard was not so lucky. During a battle with two pursuing ships, the legendary pirate was killed by a gunshot when the authorities boarded his ship.

Only Blackbeard knew the secret location of his vast treasure hidden in the tidal marsh west of Charleston, and that knowledge died with him on the ocean.

The Charleston tidal marsh also held considerable appeal for another pirate, Stede Bonnet. Bonnet was not as flamboyant as Blackbeard and is somewhat less well known, but in his day he was considered to be the greatest terror of the high seas. Originally a successful farmer and businessman from the island of Barbados, Bonnet longed for adventure most of his life—a longing not satisfied by the farming and marketing of sugar cane. Bonnet eventually sold off large portions of his estate, purchased a seaworthy sloop which he named the *Revenge,* and had it fitted with several large cannons and manned by a crew of seventy of some of the most bloodthirsty cutthroats he could find on the island.

One day, Bonnet sailed the *Revenge* from the Barbados port of Bridgetown, and thereafter devoted himself to raiding and plundering ships in both the Caribbean Sea and the Atlantic Ocean. After only a few months, Bonnet and his crew had accumulated several million dollars' worth of gold bullion and coins.

Bonnet, like Blackbeard, was attracted to the port of Charleston, and following a series of successful raids along the Atlantic seaboard, he would put in at this South Carolina haven and enjoy the peaceful life he found there. Also like Blackbeard, Bonnet found the tidal marsh an ideal place in which to conceal his abundant wealth. After landing at the busy port, Bonnet, with the aid of several of his henchmen, would load wooden chests filled with purloined treasure into a rowboat under cover of night, disappear into the marsh to bury the loot, and return the next morning.

It is believed by most researchers of the Stede Bonnet story that the pirate was never able to retrieve what must have been a tremendous fortune secreted in the tidal marshes, for he was eventually captured, tried, found guilty of several crimes, and hanged, along with twenty-nine of his crew members, in Charleston. As with Blackbeard, the knowledge of the location of Stede Bonnet's treasure hidden in the nearby tidal marsh was carried with him to his grave.

A third pirate who realized the advantages of the tidal marshes for hiding treasure was undoubtedly one of the most unusual buccaneers to sail the seas. Mary Anne Townsend was the niece of a prominent government official in Jamestown when she met the infamous pirate, Blackbeard. A passenger on the Shropshire Lass as it was leaving Bermuda, the very attractive Townsend, along with crew members and other passengers, was surprised by a sudden attack from Blackbeard and his men. Townsend watched in horror as the pirate leader killed many of her fellow travelers, and was shocked, yet strangely fascinated, when he forced several to walk the plank.

When it came Townsend's turn to be executed, she fought her tormentors, spit in their faces, and cursed and berated them loudly, daring them to lay a hand on her. Standing six feet tall with flaming red hair and the spirit of a tigress, she was not intimidated by the ruffians and held them at bay. Attracted by the commotion, Blackbeard approached and for the first time gazed upon the beauty of Mary Anne Townsend. Quite uncharacteristically, the famous pirate bowed low before the brave woman and personally escorted her to a private cabin in the hold of his own ship.

Blackbeard, obviously quite taken with the fiery Townsend, began to court her. He gave her jewels, gold, silks, and satins, all of which were of course stolen. He promised her a life of wealth, adventure, and luxury if she would only follow him. Intrigued by this charismatic pirate, and possessing a barely concealed lust for adventure herself, Mary Anne Townsend committed herself to a life of piracy at that point.

Throwing herself into her new role, she encouraged Blackbeard to teach her all that he knew, and the two made a most amazing pair of brigands.

After several months of apprenticing with Blackbeard, Townsend obtained her own vessel, which she named the *Odyssey*. She had no difficulty assembling a competent crew of sailors and freebooters, and soon she was attacking and pillaging ships in the Atlantic Ocean with abandon.

In addition to teaching her the fine points of piracy, Blackbeard also introduced Townsend to the wonders and pleasures of Charleston. During their times together in this port, the two would often go from tavern to tavern, drinking ale, laughing, and exchanging tales with other pirates.

While resting with their crews in Charleston one summer, Blackbeard informed Townsend of his secret hiding place in the tidal marsh, and advised her to consider a similar method of caching her wealth. Together, the two pirates often guided several rowboats filled with booty into the forbidden interior of the marsh where they supervised the burial. It has been estimated by historians that Townsend, like Blackbeard and Bonnet, concealed millions of dollars' worth of gold and silver coins and bullion, jewels, and precious artifacts in the marsh.

Several months later, Townsend was busily attacking, pillaging, and sinking merchant ships in the Caribbean Sea when she received news of the death of her mentor, Blackbeard. On putting into port at Jamaica several days later, Townsend also learned that government authorities had offered a huge reward for her capture, dead or alive. She was informed that ships were on the way into the Caribbean at that very moment in pursuit of her.

Townsend immediately equipped the *Odyssey* with stores and provisions and set sail for South America, where she believed she would be safe. The only treasure she carried with her was that which had been obtained from her most recent raids. The bulk of her huge fortune still lay concealed in the Charleston tidal marsh, approximately 1,600 miles away in South Carolina.

Stories of what became of Mary Anne Townsend during the ensuing years were numerous and widespread, but none was ever verified. The most prevalent tale related that she eventually arrived in Lima, Peru, married a wealthy Spaniard, and happily lived out the rest of her life in luxury.

Other pirates were known to have used the Charleston tidal marsh as a location to hide their booty, but by far the largest hoards belonged to Blackbeard, Bonnet, and Townsend. While no one ever knew the exact locations of these hiding places, it was common knowledge around Charleston that millions of dollars' worth of treasure were deposited there.

Over the years, numerous efforts have been made to locate the various pirate caches, but the tidal marsh presents a formidable hiding place. Snakes, mosquitoes, and other varieties of swamp vermin are an incessant annoyance to the searcher, and the possibilities of getting lost in the region are great.

Interest in the pirates' hidden caches has not lessened over the years. Even today, treasure hunters by the dozens enter the marsh, armed with sophisticated metal detectors and other equipment, and each believes he will be the one to locate one of the hiding places and recover the pirate caches.

Found:
The Long-lost Treasure
of the SS Central America

During a two week period of time in the summer of 1857, the huge paddle wheel steamer SS *Central America* lay at anchor in a San Francisco Bay harbor. For several days teams of laborers loaded an incredibly rich cargo onto the boat—three tons of gold! The gold represented the monthly shipment from the San Francisco mint to several New York banks, and at today's exchange rates this gold would likely be worth in excess of 450 million dollars.

In addition to the huge cargo of minted gold, at least a dozen individuals who had made fortunes in the rich California gold fields were returning to the East with their personal wealth—fortunes in the form of gold bars and gold coins.

When the rich cargo was finally loaded, the SS *Central America* steamed out of San Francisco Bay on a lengthy journey that was to take it down the west coast of North America, through the Isthmus of Panama, and then up the eastern seaboard to the city of New York, where the passengers would be dropped off and the gold unloaded.

As the SS *Central America* made the slow voyage toward the Empire State, it encountered the leading edge of a hurricane some two hundred miles off the coast of South

Carolina. Underestimating the power of what was to become an incredibly fierce storm, the captain of the steamship decided to continue on to New York rather than seek refuge along the South Carolina coast. It was a decision that would ultimately cost many lives and lead to one of the most prolonged searches for a sunken ship in the history of North America.

As the storm raged, the steamship was repeatedly buffeted by the choppy waters, throwing crew, passengers, and cargo all about. Though huge and somewhat stout, the SS *Central America* was clumsy and difficult to control in anything but calm seas. It was certainly not built to withstand the severe storm conditions to which it was now being subjected. After fighting the hurricane for several hours, the steamship began to break apart and ultimately went down in about eight thousand feet of ocean. Once the vessel began taking on water, it was just a matter of a few minutes before it and its entire cargo disappeared from the surface and sank to the sandy bottom of the continental shelf. A total of 425 people perished. There were 153 survivors who, clinging to broken timbers and life rafts, drifted on the sea until they were rescued several days later.

For over a century, researchers believed the SS *Central America* had been blown northward by the storm for at least a hundred miles before sinking, placing its grave somewhere off the coast of North Carolina. During dozens of attempted recovery expeditions, divers braved the extreme depths of this part of the Atlantic Ocean bottom in search of the lost steamer, hoping to locate some of the treasure known to be on board. The SS *Central America,* however, remained elusive, and every effort made to locate it ended in failure.

In 1986, an organization called the Columbus America Discovery Group, operating out of Columbus, Ohio, claimed they had found the wreck. After several months of intensive searching, they discovered what they believed to be the SS *Central America* some two hundred miles off the coast of South Carolina and well over a hundred miles from the previously suspected site of the sinking. For nearly two years, the Columbus America group probed and dug into and around the wreck in an attempt to determine its true identity. In 1988, all doubts concerning the identification of the vessel were erased when the ship's bell was finally brought to the surface.

Once they were certain they had located the SS *Central America,* the group invested a great deal of time, effort, and money in making preparations to salvage the treasure, and the first gold bars and artifacts were brought up in August of 1989.

What the salvors found would make the eyes of the most experienced and hardened treasure hunter bulge. Several gold bars weighing sixty-two pounds apiece were retrieved, with the promise of many more to come. Rare, double-eagle gold coins valued at up to twenty thousand dollars each were discovered, along with several privately minted gold coins estimated to be worth fifteen thousand dollars apiece.

When asked about the potential worth of the total find once it is all recovered, members of the Columbus America group said it could likely amount to one billion dollars!

While figures on the amount of gold shipped by the San Francisco mint are documented, less is known of the quantities of gold bars and coins carried aboard the steamer by passengers. The value of these, according to the recovery group, will depend on the quality of what is found along with its rarity and demand.

Most of the gold and artifacts are being recovered through the use of advanced technology—a computer-based imaging system that allows the searchers to see far below the surface where the old steamship lies. This is augmented by an underwater vehicle equipped with cameras and a high-precision robotic arm capable of picking up small objects.

The story of the SS *Central America* is an excellent case study of a lost treasure that has been recovered as the result of persistent and careful research aided by state-of-the-art equipment. The techniques employed and refined during this discovery and retrieval process, along with that of other similar deep ocean excavations and recoveries that are currently taking place, will undoubtedly be employed to locate, investigate, and raise treasures and artifacts from the hundreds of other sunken vessels that litter the floors of the continental shelves of North America.

The Indian Gold Mine de Soto Never Found

One of the most fascinating and enduring lost mine legends in South Carolina tells of a rich lode of gold known to the local Indians and at one time sought by the famed Spanish explorer Hernando de Soto. The mine, probably in present-day Pickens County, was never found by the intrepid de Soto, and for centuries it was apparently a primary source of the gold used by several area Indian tribes to make fine jewelry, ornaments, and icons.

As de Soto traveled and explored the southern Appalachians, he thought always of his mission to locate, excavate, and ship back to Spain any and all kinds of precious metals. When he stumbled across a gold or silver mine operated by Indians, he would often enslave the members of the tribe and force them to dig the ore for Spain. If the Indians resisted, de Soto would kill several of the tribe's leaders as an example. Thus, the gold-hungry Spaniard subjugated, tortured, and killed hundreds of Indians in his quest for wealth for the Spanish king.

At an Indian village called Nepetaca in what is now southern Georgia, a young Indian who was about to be tortured by de Soto's men pleaded for mercy, telling his captors he knew of a wealthy gold mine in the mountains several marches to the north. The mine was supposed to be a three-day ride from a large Indian village called Cofitachiqui, which was ruled by a queen.

The soldiers brought the young man to de Soto, and the explorer listened with interest to the story. He decided to go to Cofitachiqui, and ordered his men to get ready to leave immediately. De Soto had one of his priests baptize the young Indian, gave him the Christian name of Peter, and incorporated him into his army.

The Spanish force left Nepetaca in March, 1540, and for several weeks traveled north through the plains, forests, and swamps of the humid lowlands. Provisions were running dangerously low, hunting was poor, and the progress and morale of the party was deteriorating rapidly. Whenever the Spaniards sighted an Indian village, they would prepare to raid it for food and women only to find each time it was infested with smallpox brought to the region by an earlier Spanish explorer, Vasquez de Ayllon. De Soto's army gave each such village a wide berth.

Several times, de Soto was ready to abandon the quest for the mine, but young Peter always reassured him that the waiting riches would make the toil and sacrifices worthwhile.

But after weeks of weary marching and being forced to eat dogs and horses, an angry and frustrated de Soto ordered the young Indian killed. Juan Ortiz, de Soto's chief interpreter, argued for Peter's life, saying that the boy's knowledge of the local language would prove useful and could mean the difference between life and death. De Soto relented, and four days later, the young Indian led the party of Spaniards to the outskirts of Cofitachiqui.

The village lay spread along the flood plain of the Savannah River about a dozen miles downstream from present-day Augusta, Georgia, on the South Carolina side of the river. The village housed large families in its many circular earthen structures, and had been spared the smallpox epidemic that had decimated tribes farther south.

The inhabitants of Cofitachiqui were friendly, cultured, and courteous.

As de Soto and his men rode into the village, they were warmly greeted by the Indians and invited to a welcoming feast. The Spaniards were brought gifts of fresh-water pearls, fine furs, and food.

Looking around at the Indian population, de Soto noticed much gold. Many of the Indians were wearing armbands, rings, and ornate headpieces made from it.

During the feast, the queen of the village came to the Spanish leader. De Soto wrote in his journals that the queen was tall, almost statuesque, light of color, and very attractive. De Soto called the queen *la Señora,* and he thanked her when she personally welcomed the Spaniards and invited them to set up camp near the village.

Playing the role of the grateful guest, de Soto agreed to remain for a few days, but uppermost in his mind was gold. A casual walk through the Indian village revealed that the dwellings and temples were filled with gold icons and ornaments. De Soto even saw ceremonial ax blades and spearheads made from the precious metal.

He asked for and was granted an audience with *la Señora,* and during their conversation, he asked where the wealth he saw in the village had come from. The queen would not be specific, but did tell the Spaniard that for many generations the Indians had excavated gold from a mine in the mountains to the north. She claimed the mine had an unending supply of the precious ore and would provide the metal for her people for centuries to come.

That evening, greed overtaking gratitude, de Soto made plans to kidnap *la Señora* and force her to guide him to the mine.

At dawn the following day, the Spanish soldiers swarmed into the village, sacked the temples, and seized the queen and several of her followers. De Soto told *la Señora* that she was to guide him and his army to the rich gold mine in the north or they would all be tortured and killed. The queen and her followers agreed to show the Spaniard the mine, and the party began to wind its way through the low foothills of western South Carolina toward the higher reaches of the mountains looming miles ahead of them.

Progress was slowed dramatically when spring rains struck the second day of the journey. Torrents fell for days on the Spanish army and its captives, making travel nearly impossible at times. Flood waters washed out trails, and the company got lost more than once. Rivers were often too high and swift to ford, forcing the travelers to wait days to cross. The horses were slowed by the soft muck of the trails.

Word had spread to Indian villages north of Cofitachiqui that the queen had been taken by the Spaniards, and each time the army approached a village, they were met with hostility and sometimes attacked. Several soldiers were killed, food again became scarce, and de Soto's confidence began to suffer.

The journey that was to take only days dragged into weeks. The Spaniards were weary and frustrated, and de Soto was beginning to worry about dissension. The soldiers were tired of difficult marching and going days without food. The men guarding the queen and her subordinates grew more careless each day, and one evening, *la Señora* and her follwers saw their chance and escaped.

De Soto, having lost his hostage and guide to the rich gold mine, became discouraged and surly. Fearing he would soon lose control of his army, he ordered them to abandon the quest. Turning their backs on the Appalachian Mountains, the party of explorers marched west toward the lowlands, reaching the Mississippi River many weeks later.

Scholars, prospectors, geologists, and students of this tale of a lost gold mine in the South Carolina Appalachians have often debated whether the lode really exists, but some facts support that it does. First, there *was* an abundance of gold in the village of Cofitachiqui. Second, the Indians had little reason for lying about the source of the ore, for to them it was used merely for ornaments and ceremony and had no value as a medium of exchange. Third, gold has been found elsewhere in the South Carolina Appalachians. There are impressive deposits in both Pickens and York Counties.

De Soto was probably only a day or two from the famed Indian gold mine of the Appalachians, but the hardship of his journey, coupled with the escape of his prisoners, caused him to abandon the quest.

The incident was the first of the difficulties and bad luck that would plague the Spanish leader. While his party did cross the wide Mississippi River and find gold in the Ozark and Ouachita Mountains to the west, de Soto's health was starting to deteriorate. Many of his soldiers deserted, several with fortunes in gold and silver gained in the expedition. Eventually de Soto became delirious and had to be carried on a litter. The Spaniard, an important early explorer of the southern United States, died somewhere near the Arkansas-Louisiana border while trying to get back to Spain.

The lost mine of the South Carolina Appalachians was said to be a rich source of almost pure gold for the local Indians, who were probably members of the Creek tribe. When the area was abandoned during the infamous Trail of Tears resettlement, the mine was closed and probably covered over. Many have searched for it over the past century and a half, yet it remains lost.

Sunken Art Treasures in the Atlantic

For generations, great art has been prized and coveted by many of the world's wealthy, and a large number of the fabulous art treasures stolen from museums and private collections in Europe have made their way into the hands of American collectors willing to pay exhorbitant prices for them.

The selling of valuable, stolen art objects on the black market has been a lucrative endeavor for many, but huge profits were also made by the ship captains who transported these items from Europe to the New World.

One such character was a colorful privateer named Allen Winslow. As a youth, he was taken aboard a pirate ship where he labored for years, eventually acquiring the status of a well-respected seaman and fighter. While serving with several well known pirates of the day, Winslow became fascinated by the fortunes that could be made raiding ships on the open sea. In time, he commanded his own pirate vessel and is said to have amassed incredible wealth roaming the North Atlantic ocean and plundering treasure-laden ships flying the flag of Spain.

While relaxing in London in 1810 following several months at sea, Winslow learned of the growing traffic in stolen art. Here, he reasoned, was a way of life that could be almost as profitable as pirating and considerably safer.

He let it be known that he was willing to transport stolen art across the Atlantic to customers in America, and soon found himself in demand.

Winslow acquired an out-of-service United States Navy gunboat, the *Beaufort,* which fit his purposes nicely. It was a fifty-foot-long sailing vessel that had outlived its usefulness as a warship. Light and maneuverable, the speedy little *Beaufort* was more than adequate to efficiently and effectively transport light loads of stolen art treasures.

Following the actual theft, the most hazardous part of trafficking in stolen art objects was the delivery of the goods at the prescribed destination point. Many smugglers have been captured as they attempted to unload fortunes in paintings and statuary at American ports. Winslow was an expert at delivering his precious cargo, preferring to arrive during the night, have his well-trained crew rapidly unload the contraband for the waiting customer, and quickly sail away before sunrise.

Winslow set up his base of operations on Grand Bahama Island near the Florida coast, where he received stolen goods from England brought by other ships which he had commissioned for the purpose. Once the shipments were transferred to the *Beaufort,* Winslow quickly delivered the goods to various destinations along the Atlantic coast and picked up a hefty fee for himself.

One summer afternoon Winslow set sail for the port of New York. Inside the ship's hold were numerous place settings of the finest silverware, silvered mirrors crafted of exquisite Venetian glass, several priceless oil paintings by recognized masters, silver and gold candelabras, and jewelry fashioned from the world's finest diamonds, emeralds, and pearls.

Winslow's normal routine was to cross the western Atlantic from Grand Bahama Isle to Cape Hatteras on the North Carolina coast and then proceed to a certain destination, usually New York. Because of a storm brewing in the Atlantic along his accustomed route, Winslow decided instead to sail directly to Florida and follow the coastline northward. Should he encounter the storm, he could simply anchor the *Beaufort* in the calmer waters of a coastal estuary and wait out the storm.

For several days, Winslow successfully piloted the *Beaufort* up the Atlantic coastline, passing the larger seaside settlements during the night in order to avoid detection. Though the storm continued to rage, its nucleus was still many miles away in open waters and, aside from rough waters, posed no immediate threat to the *Beaufort*.

One morning, having successfully sailed past the South Carolina port of Charleston during the night, Captain Winslow and his crew began to relax, when a lookout suddenly alerted them to the presence of a federal gunboat about a mile off starboard. As he strained to see the oncoming cutter, Winslow ordered his men to ready the cannons.

The speed of the cutter, superior to that of the *Beaufort*, told Winslow that his only chance, if challenged, would be to fight. He could not allow his ship full of stolen goods to be boarded and inspected.

As the cutter drew alongside the *Beaufort*, Winslow prepared to give the command to fire—when suddenly the captain of the federal boat challenged Winslow to a race!

Surprised and relieved, Winslow readily agreed and the crews of both vessels readied their sails. As the two boats picked up speed and raced northeastward, the threatening storm moved landward and generated impressively large swells in the relatively shallow coastal waters. Winslow noted that the portside coastline was approximately one mile distant.

The two ships raced for more than twenty miles, the cutter maintaining a slight edge, when the winds suddenly increased and the crew of the *Beaufort* were unable to hold their course. Winslow ordered his sailors to drop the mainsail in order to regain control, but he had no sooner shouted the command when the mainmast snapped, causing the ship to veer sharply. The strain of the sudden movement was too much for the vessel, and several of the bow plankings snapped, opening up a large hole. Sea water surged in and within seconds the *Beaufort* disappeared beneath the choppy waters, carrying with it a fortune in precious art objects.

Minutes later, the federal cutter returned to pick up the survivors. Winslow and his crew were transported to Charleston where, much to his surprise, the smuggler received an official apology from the United States government and reimbursement for the loss of his ship.

Winthin weeks, Winslow resumed ferrying stolen art to American buyers, but neither he nor anyone else ever made an attempt to recover the fortune in art objects that went down with the *Beaufort.*

According to Winslow, the *Beaufort* sank just a few moments after passing the northeastern tip of Bull Island. After picking the survivors out of the sea, the captain of the federal cutter, reacting to the impending severe weather, immediately steered the vessel due west into the calmer water of adjacent Bull's Bay.

Because the *Beaufort* was loaded with illegal contraband, neither Winslow nor his employers left any written record of the route taken, the encounter with the federal ship, or the loss of the *Beaufort.* Consequently, the exact offshore location of the wreck is unknown.

Millions of dollars' worth of art objects are believed to still lie within the rotted hold of the *Beaufort,* resting on the sea floor perhaps only a mile from South Carolina's Bull Island.

Bullion and Arms
Off North Island

History is filled with accounts of shipwrecks along the Atlantic coast of the United States. Many of the ships that have gone down during the past three hundred years were carrying treasure—great cargoes of gold and silver bullion and coins, chests filled with precious stones and jewels, gold and silver ingots, individual and corporate funds.

During American's Civil War, a curious cargo carried by a foreign ship on a clandestine mission was lost beneath the waves of the Atlantic Ocean near the South Carolina coast.

When the War Between the States began in 1861, England maintained an official position of neutrality while secretly supporting the South. As the war raged on, many British citizens as well as government representatives quietly aligned themselves with the philosophies of the secessionist Confederacy. In addition, several important and influential British industrialists had large investments in the American South, and so it was in their best interests to support the Rebel cause. As a result, several organizations were formed in England to contribute arms and money to the Southern effort and to carry on an active supply program for the Confederates.

The British provided ships and guns to the Rebels on a regular basis until the arrangement was discovered by

Union forces. Thereafter, Yankee warships regularly patroled the coast between Virginia and Florida, constantly on the lookout for British vessels. The Union boats sailed as far as the West Indies where, at one point, they actually detained a British vessel. This incident became known as the Trent Affair, and it nearly precipitated a war between Great Britain and the United States.

During the War Between the States, as many as thirty British ships were regularly crossing and recrossing the Atlantic Ocean, carrying supplies and funds to the Southerners. Many of these ships encountered Union blockades, but several managed to reach port somewhere along the coast and deliver their cargo.

In April of 1863, the British warship *York Castle* lay quietly moored to a London dock. For three full days and nights, the crew of both British and American sailors prepared the ship for a trans-Atlantic voyage and, contrary to official British policy, loaded a secret cargo bound for the Southern states into the hull. The shipment, contributed by one of the British organizations in sympathy with the Confederate cause, consisted of 350,000 dollars in gold ingots, 1,300 Enfield rifles, two dozen kegs of black powder, and numerous crates of ammunition. When all was ready, the *York Castle* quietly slipped from the harbor and out into the open waters of the Atlantic.

The *York Castle* was a corvette, a small, fast warship. The advantage of such a lightweight vessel was its speed, a crucial factor in evading Union blockades and outrunning pursuing ships. Because of its small size, however, a corvette normally carried only a few lightweight cannons—a distinct disadvantage in a sea battle with larger ships.

Days later the *York Castle* arrived in the Bahamas and took on fresh food and water. During the Civil War the Bahama Islands, an archipelago in the Atlantic Ocean just southeast of Florida, were a convenient stopover point for British supply ships to replenish food and water and rest their crews. Recent information concerning the activities of the Union warships was often available there.

While the *York Castle* lay at dock at Grand Bahama Island, its captain learned from other British blockade runners that most of the Yankee vessels had been pulled out of Southern waters. After remaining in port for two days, the *York Castle* set sail for Virginia, where a contingent of Rebel soldiers awaited the gold and weapons.

Off the east coast of Florida the fast little ship sailed northward, hugging the shore. Should a Union warship be spotted, the corvette was capable of sailing up relatively shallow estuaries, thereby evading confrontation.

For several days the *York Castle* appeared to be the only ship in Atlantic waters. As the corvette crossed Winyah Bay between South Carolina's North Island and South Island, two Union ships appeared suddenly and without warning, tacking along the continent-side coast of North Island. The captain of the *York Castle* decided to try to outrun the federal boats, but they were cutters and, like the corvette, were swift and maneuverable on the open sea.

Realizing that the *York Castle* would soon be overtaken, the captain positioned the vessel to fire its cannons at the oncoming cutters. The first volley struck one of the cutters and rendered it useless for battle, but the other cutter returned fire and succeeded in destroying the corvette's tall mast. The heavy sails, now on fire, tumbled down onto the deck. As the *York Castle* continued to fire on the Union cutters, the foredeck broke out in flames. Within minutes, the ship was ablaze and the crew members were frantically jumping into the ocean.

Soon the flames reached the black powder stored in the hull, resulting in a tremendous explosion which lifted the *York Castle* almost entirely out of the water. The front of the ship had been completely blown away, and shattered planks and timbers were hurled into the sea for more than a hundred yards in all directions. The ruined vessel slammed back down onto the surface of the water, perched

169

at an odd list for several seconds, and then slowly took on water and sank beneath the waves, carrying the 350,000 dollars in gold ingots and the 1,300 Enfield rifles to the bottom.

The captain of the *York Castle* was killed in the blast but the Yankee cutters managed to rescue about thirty survivors of the explosion, all of whom were taken to the nearest port and placed under arrest.

For years very few people were aware of the rich cargo that was being transported by the *York Castle*. The British vessel was considered nothing more than just another casualty of the war, and was soon forgotten.

While examining some obscure documents in England during the 1920s, a researcher uncovered information about the mission and cargo of the *York Castle*. After verifying the data, he decided to attempt to salvage the treasure.

An expedition was organized and within months the continental shelf east of North Island was searched for the sunken, treasure-laden corvette. Because the exact location of the *York Castle's* demise was unknown, the salvage team conducted a systematic grid search of the sea floor near North Island; however, heavy storms encroached on the region, causing them to abandon their project. For weeks the seas remained choppy and hazardous. Finally, depleted of funds and patience, the expedition team returned to England.

History records no other attempts to locate the remains of the *York Castle*. If the vessel can ever be located, its finders stand a good chance of retrieving a fortune in gold and antique rifles.

TENNESSEE

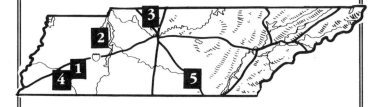

1. Treasure in the Well
2. Unrecovered Yankee Gold
3. The Lost Gold of the Recluse
4. Buried Cache of Silver Dollars
5. Buried Kegs of Gold and Silver Coins

Treasure in the Well

In southwestern Madison County there is a piece of land that oldtimers sometimes still refer to as the Old Fuller Place. Artie Fuller, who purchased hundreds of acres in the region prior to the War Between the States, was a successful cotton farmer, owned a luxurious plantation house, and was reputed to be the wealthiest man in western Tennessee. As Fuller's fortune from his cotton-growing operation grew, so did his distrust of banks, and he eventually began storing his wealth in one of the mansion's closets.

Fuller, a middle-aged man with no children, always insisted that payment for his cotton crop be made in gold coin, and as his harvests were bountiful and his profits high, the mansion closet was soon filled with canvas sacks containing twenty-dollar gold pieces.

As the Civil War raged throughout much of the South, Madison County was spared many of the horrors inflicted on other places. Although Union and Confederate soldiers were often seen riding through the region, Madison County citizens were by and large unmolested. Experiencing no interference whatsoever, Fuller, with the help of his many slaves, was able to pursue the operation of the cotton plantation. Artie Fuller was a die-hard Southerner who considered the war a temporary nuisance. He staunchly supported the Confederacy and believed that the Rebel forces would eventually prevail, the hated Yankees would be driven from the region, and life would soon return to normal.

On the morning of June 10, 1864, Fuller's wife, Jesse, insisted he find a new location for his gold-filled canvas sacks, as she needed the space in the closet for other things. With the help of one of his slaves, Fuller hauled the sacks out onto the front porch of the mansion with the intention of selecting a suitable location somewhere on the grounds in which to bury them.

As he was considering this, a rider, furiously whipping his mount, approached the mansion and warned Fuller of approaching Union soldiers. The frantic plantation owner did not want the Yankees to see his gold, for he knew they would confiscate it. In the few minutes before the troops arrived, Fuller and the slave carried the sacks to the nearby well and tossed them in. Just as the last sack splashed into the deep waters, a group of some fifteen uniformed men was spotted riding up the path toward the house.

As they approached, Fuller realized that the newcomers were not soldiers, but bandits. Though clothed in the uniforms of Union troops, this ragtag gang of scruffy outlaws, like many others of the time, made a living by raiding and robbing area farms and small towns, often torturing and killing many citizens in the process.

Fuller recognized the group's leader. Fielding Hurst, a bloodthirsty cutthroat wanted by both armies as well as by several area law enforcement agencies, had served with both the Union and Confederate forces. His record with the Confederacy was spotty and he was currently regarded as a deserter by the Yankees. Hurst was well known throughout western Tennessee as a result of his exploits. Fuller felt he would have had a better chance against a real contingent of Yankee soldiers than against this outlaw.

After ordering his wife, maid, and cook to take shelter in the cellar, Fuller grabbed a shotgun and walked out onto the porch to face the bandits. Summoning all of his courage, he sternly ordered the outlaws off his property, pointing the shotgun directly at Hurst.

Sitting astride his horse, the bandit leader distracted Fuller with conversation while two members of the gang silently crept up on the farmer from behind. At a signal from Hurst, the two outlaws jumped Fuller, wrestled the weapon from his grasp, and flung him to the ground.

Dismounting, Hurst walked over to Fuller and demanded he turn over his fortune immediately. When the farmer refused, Hurst kicked him several times in the ribs and told him he would be killed unless he revealed the location of his wealth.

When Fuller continued to refuse, Hurst threatened to hang him. Fuller ignored the outlaw's threats and defiantly ordered him to be on his way. Enraged, Hurst had two men drag Fuller to a nearby tree where a noose was secured around his neck and the other end of the rope thrown over a stout limb. At a command from Hurst, several of the bandits pulled on the trailing end of the rope and lifted the farmer several feet off the ground. Fuller fought the tightening noose with a fury and energy that belied his age. For several minutes he kicked and bucked against the rope, but eventually passed out. Just as Fuller was about to strangle, Hurst ordered his men to release the rope and the farmer dropped to the ground, barely alive. When Fuller regained consciousness after several minutes, the outlaw leader once again demanded to know the whereabouts of his fortune. When he could finally speak, Fuller looked the bandit directly in the eye and told him to go to hell.

For a second time Fuller was hoisted up to dangle from the tree limb, the ever-tightening noose constricting his windpipe. And again, when his struggles ceased and he seemed on the point of death, he was lowered to the ground. Hurst gave Fuller one last chance to reveal the location of his gold, but the plucky farmer merely shook his head and rasped a defiance. For a third time, Hurst ordered Fuller pulled up, and this time he let him hang until he was dead.

As two of the outlaws tied off the rope and left the dead plantation owner swinging from the tree limb, the rest of them, led by Hurst, ransacked the house. For several hours they searched the mansion, the barn, and the grounds, but found none of Fuller's money. Miraculously, Jesse Fuller and the other women hiding in the cellar went undiscovered by the bandits.

When several hours had passed and it was apparent that the bandits had departed, Mrs. Fuller came out from hiding. She found her husband hanging from the tree in the front yard and immediately had him cut down and buried.

For three weeks, Jesse Fuller remained on the plantation pondering her future. Finally, she decided she could no longer stay in Madison County and made arrangements to move in with her sister in Holly Springs, Mississippi.

While making preparations to leave the area, Jesse Fuller would visit the well several times a day and peer into its depths as if wondering what to do about the great fortune hidden there. A few days before departing for Mississippi, she asked the slaves fill the shaft and remove all evidence of the existence of the well. When her neighbors asked why she did such a thing, she refused to discuss the matter and quickly changed the subject. Many years later when she was asked the same question, Mrs. Fuller told the story of the hiding of the gold, and merely stated that the money belonged to her husband and no one else should have it.

In spite of her wishes, others apparently felt they were entitled to at least try to locate Fuller's treasure, and the abandoned farm was visited often over the next several years by treasure hunters who searched the mansion and excavated numerous holes in the the yard.

Long neglected and in a state of considerable disrepair, the Fuller mansion was torn down in 1921. Although the old house had been searched time and again, the occasion of its razing was attended by many who poked about the foundation and debris for any sign of Fuller's gold coins.

A few years later, the true account of the money hidden in the well was being told around this part of the South, and soon hundreds of the curious flocked to the old Fuller plantation in the hope of discovering the location of the old well; but so much time had passed that no one was left alive who had any idea where it was originally located.

Unrecovered Yankee Gold

During the American Civil War, both Confederate and Union forces were constantly on the move throughout much of Tennessee. Along with men, horses and mules, wagons, supplies, and artillery, the armies normally transported a military payroll which was often paid out to the soldiers while on the march. At any given time during the Civil War, millions of dollars, usually in gold coin, were in transit from one skirmish to another.

During the last few weeks of 1862, Union colonel C.L. Dunham, commander of the 39th Iowa Division, led his mounted troops and foot soldiers into western Tennessee in the hope of engaging the Seventh Tennessee Cavalry led by General Nathan Bedford Forrest. On December 29th, the Union division marched through the small settlement of Huntington, heading south.

Confederate leader Forrest and his soldiers had experienced considerable success in recent battles throughout this part of the South. The latest intelligence reports revealed that Forrest's army was camped at Parker's Crossroads, about fifteen miles due south of Huntington. Dunham received specific orders from General Grant to proceed to this location, where he was to engage and defeat the enemy.

By the time Dunham's command reached Clarksburg, approximately ten miles south of Huntington, the sun had set. A suitable location to camp for the night was found near a fresh-water spring just outside of town; Dunham ordered a halt, and within minutes horses and mules were hobbled and tents were set up.

Early the following morning, Union scouts reported to Dunham that Forrest's command was, in fact, camped at Parker's Crossroads about five miles to the south. The scouts noted that Forrest had anticipated the arrival of Dunham's forces, for the Confederates were digging trenches and making other battle preparations.

Forgoing breakfast, Dunham's men readied their weapons and horses for the march to Parker's Crossroads. As the troops prepared for the coming encounter, Dunham gave thought to the payroll chest filled with gold coins, estimated to have been in excess of 15,000 dollars. Not wishing to risk loss or capture of the Union Army payroll, he decided to bury it nearby, intending to return for it after engaging Forrest. With the aid of two trusted lieutenants and a sergeant, Dunham alternately carried and dragged the heavy chest to a location approximately 200 feet east of the spring. Here a hole was dug and the chest was lowered into it and covered.

Unseen by the four men, a Union scout named Allen Chambliss squatted on a knoll overlooking the excavation site. As he cleaned his rifle, Chambliss witnessed the caching of the payroll chest. This made a total of five men who knew the location of the buried coins.

All day long, Dunham's army advanced slowly and cautiously on the Confederates. By nightfall the Yankees could see the Confederate camp, but Dunham did not wish to engage the well-entrenched enemy in the dark. Members of the 39th Iowa Division got little sleep that night as they remained poised only a few hundred yards from the Rebel camp.

On the morning of December 31, the first shots were fired and the battle was on. For nearly a full day the two armies fought bitterly, with both sides incurring heavy casualties. Forrest's command was greatly outnumbered by the Yankees, but the cunning general managed to create significant confusion and damage. Having accomplished all he believed was possible against Dunham's superior numbers, Forrest ordered his forces to retreat from the battle site and the Rebels fled southwestward, eventually crossing the Tennessee River near the town of Clifton.

At Parker's Crossroads, nearly a hundred men, both Union and Confederate, lay dead on the field of battle. Hundreds more had suffered serious wounds, and for the next few days and nights the army surgeons were busy treating the injured while squads of enlisted men buried the dead. Dunham watched sadly as the two lieutenants and the sergeant who had helped him bury the gold-filled chest were lowered into the ground.

On the morning after the battle, a week of heavy rains began to fall, impeding the treatment of the wounded and the burying of the dead.

Among those recovering in one of the army tents was Allen Chambliss. Chambliss had been struck by a Rebel bullet during the first few minutes of the battle, lost a great deal of blood, and at first was mistakenly pronounced dead. Several days later he regained consciousness, and the doctors believed his chances for recovery were good.

By the second day of the downpour, the battlefield had turned into a quagmire and movement was restricted. On the morning of the sixth day after the battle, Dunham gathered a contingent of six well-armed men and a wagon and rode back up the trail toward Clarksburg, intending to retrieve the payroll chest.

Twice they were forced to abandon the trail and hide from oncoming Rebel patrols. When they were just two miles outside of Clarksburg, a third enemy patrol opened fire on them, killing two of the Union soldiers. Finally, frustrated by both the weather and the Confederates, Dunham decided to abandon the chest for the time being and return for it later.

When the rain finally let up, Dunham led his command back toward the north, where he hoped to replenish lost men, horses, and supplies. Several of the most seriously wounded, including Allen Chambliss, were left at Huntington to recover. A few days later Dunham received orders to lead an expedition to another region, and the gold-filled payroll chest was soon forgotten by everyone— everyone except Allen Chambliss.

It took three months for Chambliss to recover sufficiently from his wound. Once he was able to ride, the former scout decided to travel to Clarksburg and dig up the payroll chest. After tying his horse to a tree near the spring, the young man walked to the spot where he believed the chest had been buried, but to his utter surprise, he found that the surrounding landscape had changed dramatically. Heavy runoff from the same torrential rains that had plagued the Yankees during the days following the battle had created surging streams and floodwaters, eroding away tons of topsoil in some areas and depositing it in others.

For the next several months Chambliss searched the region for the buried chest without success. Time and again he would sit atop the low hill from which he had watched the burial of the gold, but below him nothing looked the same.

Over the years, Chambliss told the tale of the buried payroll to others and, with the passage of several generations, the story has entered the realm of Tennessee folklore. While government records indicate that Dunham did indeed transport a payroll chest, Colonel Dunham's journal contains no mention of hiding it, nor was a map made of his expedition route and campground locations.

In spite of the fact that the chest was buried well over a hundred years ago, people continue to search for it. To compound the problem, however, researchers have discovered there is not just a single spring in this area, but five. Which of the springs was the one near which Dunham's command spent the night remains a mystery.

The Lost Gold of the Recluse

During the mid-1800s, large areas of the state of Tennessee were uninhabited and still considered to be a very wild and dangerous wilderness. Most newcomers to the area settled in or around the growing communities of Knoxville, Nashville, Jackson, Chattanooga, and Memphis, and only a few hardy pioneer types ventured into the remote backwoods regions to establish farms.

Sometime between 1855 and 1860, a mysterious Frenchman arrived in Nashville. Though he claimed to be a French nobleman, he had the appearance of a pauper—he wore ragged clothes, traveled on foot, and carried his meager possessions in a well-worn sack.

The man gave his name as L.S. LaPrade, and inquired around Nashville about the availability of land on which he might settle. After spending a few days in the city, LaPrade was directed to the small village of Sadlersville, about thirty-five miles northwest of Nashville.

Arriving in the Sadlersville region a few days later, LaPrade moved into an abandoned house located far from the village and surrounded by dense forest. Very few of the townspeople ever saw the newcomer, and for years the Frenchman remained reclusive, rarely coming into town. LaPrade maintained a small garden and did some trapping, and only rarely ventured into the settlement to purchase coffee and sugar at the local mercantile.

In 1875, LaPrade received a message that a relative in France had passed away and bequeathed him his entire estate—a large parcel of land and a family fortune that had belonged to the LaPrades for several generations. The Frenchman left immediately for Europe and remained gone for nearly a year. While in his home country, LaPrade sold most of the land he had inherited and withdrew large amounts of the family fortune from the banks. Once his business was completed he returned to his adopted home in America. When he left Tennessee he had lived nearly twenty years as a poor recluse. When he returned he was a very wealthy man.

LaPrade continued, however, to live in the relative squalor of his tumbledown cabin far from inquisitive neighbors. His living habits changed little except for the fact that he now hired a local black man to run errands and chop wood for him.

Andrew Duffy worked for LaPrade for nearly two years. Living with a wife and several children not far from the hermitic Frenchman, Duffy was grateful for the opportunity to earn some money and looked forward to doing chores for LaPrade. Duffy was also pleased that he was always paid with gold coins.

One afternoon when he was due to be paid, Duffy entered LaPrade's cabin without knocking and surprised the Frenchman as he was withdrawing several gold coins from a large burlap sack. Quite annoyed at being seen with his fortune, LaPrade chased Duffy from the cabin, gave him his pay, and discharged him on the spot.

Rather than depart for his home immediately, Duffy hid in the nearby forest and watched the LaPrade cabin. As he suspected, the Frenchman soon appeared at the door with his sack. Peering around to make certain he was not being watched, LaPrade dragged the heavy, gold-filled sack out into the forest opposite from where Duffy was hiding. Afraid he would be detected, Duffy remained where he was, and within twenty minutes observed LaPrade returning without the sack but with a great deal of mud on his hands and knees. Duffy deduced that LaPrade had buried the sack of coins not far from the cabin.

Over the next several days, Duffy related the incident to several of his friends, and talk of LaPrade's great wealth began to circulate in the Sadlersville area.

Some weeks later during the month of June, 1880, LaPrade needed some work done around his place and hired one William Murphy, a good friend of Andrew Duffy. Murphy, told by Duffy of the existence of the Frenchman's sack of gold coins, stayed constantly alert in the hope he might discover where it was hidden. Although he observed LaPrade closely, Murphy was unable to obtain any information concerning the whereabouts of the hidden treasure.

On the evening of August 30, Duffy, Murphy, and five friends gathered at Duffy's home and discussed the large fortune they were certain was buried near LaPrade's cabin. As the evening wore on, the men decided to force LaPrade to tell them the whereabouts of the gold. Convinced the scheme would work, the seven men left the Duffy home around midnight and went to the Frenchman's cabin.

On arriving at LaPrade's, some of the men hid in the forest and others concealed themselves behind the residence. Duffy knocked at the front door and told LaPrade he was injured and needed help. Cautiously, the Frenchman opened the door and peeked out. As the two men conversed, one of Duffy's conspirators silently crept along the front of the cabin, grabbed LaPrade, and pulled him outside.

Kicking and cursing, the Frenchman fought his attackers with determination. It eventually took four or five of them to subdue the angry man by beating him until he lost consciousness.

When LaPrade awoke several minutes later, his hands were bound tighly behind his back. Hovering over him, the seven men demanded he turn over his money to them or face serious consequences. LaPrade denied he possessed any such wealth, and repeatedly kicked at and spat upon his attackers.

LaPrade grew frantic when the men tried to hang him from a nearby tree, but the rope broke, effectively foiling this attempt at frightening the Frenchman into revealing the location of his gold.

The men then decided to torture LaPrade into revealing the location of his hidden gold. While Duffy and Murphy pinned the struggling Frenchman to the ground, two of the others severed one of the fingers from his right hand. Still the Frenchman refused to tell the men what they wanted to know, and one by one all of his fingers were removed. LaPrade's screams of agony filled the night, but so remote was the location of his cabin that he was heard by no one save his torturers.

When LaPrade continued to refuse to tell the men where his gold was hidden, his ears were cut off. Into the night, the men continued to torture the helpless recluse until LaPrade finally died from loss of blood. To the end, the Frenchman never revealed the secret location of his gold.

Fearful that their crime would be discovered, Duffy and his fellow conspirators dragged LaPrade's corpse to a nearby sinkhole and threw it in. For the next several hours before daybreak, the seven men searched the cabin and the grounds for some evidence of the large sack of gold coins but found nothing.

Ten days later, LaPrade's body was discovered in the sinkhole and Sadlersville authorities initiated an investigation into his murder.

Using extremely poor judgment, several of the attackers discussed their activities of that fateful night with friends, and before long, most of the members of the black community had been interrogated and the seven perpetrators arrested.

Duffy and Murphy agreed to testify against their five compatriots in return for their freedom. Immediately after the testimony, the two men fled the area and were never seen again. The remaining five were subsequently executed by a mob which stormed the courthouse and hanged the murderers from the balcony.

During the trial, the existence of the vast fortune in gold possessed by the Frenchman was verified, but its whereabouts remained unknown. When news of the treasure reached the public, the LaPrade cabin was searched thoroughly and torn down in the process. Dozens of holes were dug near the site but nothing of any value was ever reported found. Eventually, the story of the recluse's hidden treasure began to fade away.

Then in 1912, something happened to revive the story of the Frenchman's lost fortune.

On a remote farm located in western Arkansas, an old black man named Andrew Duffy passed away leaving nothing more than a few twenty-dollar gold pieces, several letters written in French, and a curious map that indicated the location of a buried fortune in gold near Sadlersville, Tennessee!

The area drawn on the map clearly represented the region where the LaPrade cabin once existed. Pertinent landmarks were unmistakable, and next to a small circle drawn on the map were the words, "LaPrade House." Not far from this notation were the words "gold cave."

The discovery of this map has raised many questions and answered none. Exactly how much did Andrew Duffy know of the location of LaPrade's gold? Where did he obtain these documents? Was it when he and his compatriots ransacked the Frenchman's house? And what of the allusion to a "gold cave?" Was the gold actually hidden in a cave as opposed to being buried in the ground? The region around Sadlersville contains many small caves, perhaps hundreds of them. And where did Duffy obtain the twenty-dollar gold pieces? Were they from LaPrade's hoard? Or did he earn them from honest labor after arriving in Arkansas?

More importantly, is LaPrade's huge sack filled with gold coins still hidden deep within some remote and unknown cave not far from his old homesite in the forest near Sadlersville?

Many believe it is.

Buried Cache
of Silver Dollars

Not far from the tiny settlement of Medon, Tennessee, in Hardeman County, the remains of a tumbledown cabin lie hidden in the thick brush and woods a few hundred feet from State Highway 18. This is all that is left of the home of Troy Allen, who for years operated a prosperous, three-acre truck garden that provided many of the fresh vegetables purchased by citizens for miles around. Allen, long retired, was proud of his garden, and it afforded him some extra income to supplement his meager government pension. Somewhere within the boundaries of the old garden, about two feet deep, lies a canvas sack filled with pre-1940 silver dollars, which would be worth a small fortune today.

Troy Allen was known for two things by the people of Hardeman County. They pointed to the old farmer with a sense of pride and claimed he grew the finest vegetables within a hundred miles. But as much as they liked him, everyone knew him for a miser, and many made the claim that he still possessed the first dollar he had ever made.

Allen, in truth, was a frugal man and wore the same overalls, brogans, and hat for at least twelve years straight. Between 1925 and 1940, Allen took most of his earnings to the bank in Bolivar and had it converted into silver dollars. Returning to his modest home, he would carefully

187

place the coins in a hiding place under one of the floor-boards in his bedroom.

By 1940, Allen was feeling his age and it was becoming more difficult each year for him to work in the garden. A severe case of arthritis left him almost crippled and in constant pain, and several bouts with pneumonia kept him hospitalized for weeks at a time. Allen finally decided it was time to give up farming.

On New Year's Day, 1940, Allen's daughter called and begged him to move in with her and her family in California. Allen pondered the invitation for two months, and in early March called her back to inform her he was coming, but that he needed some time to sell his small farm, close out his accounts, purchase a bus ticket, and make preparations for the long trip.

Allen's collection of silver coins, estimated to be in excess of 5,000 dollars, was far too heavy to transport to California. Though it would have been practical for the old farmer to exchange the coins for bills of large denominations, he refused, preferring instead to hold on to his silver hoard. One evening, Allen decided to hide his coins in a secret location and return for them another time. In the dark of night, he laboriously dragged the large canvas sack containing his fortune out into the middle of his beloved garden, where he buried it in a hole two feet deep. To mark the location, Allen planted a small bush on top of the cache.

During the next two weeks while he was preparing to leave, Allen told a few friends that he had hidden his fortune in silver dollars, but that he intended to return sometime in the near future to dig it up and return with it to California. Because most people considered Allen an extreme eccentric, no one paid much attention to him.

Just before he left, Allen sold his farm to a neighbor named William Myers. Myers was glad to acquire the Allen property, for it adjoined his own and he wanted to increase the size of his corn field.

Myers knew nothing of Allen's buried coins. As it was the spring of the year, Meyers was anxious to get corn planted on his new property. Two days after Allen left on the bus for California, Myers awoke early, started up his tractor, and rode it over to the old Allen place, where he plowed up the entire three-acre truck garden. The little bush marking the location of the cache of silver coins was uprooted and plowed under.

Troy Allen returned to Medon in June of the following year to retrieve his coins. Arriving at what was once his small farm, he was astonished to discover the entire acreage had been replanted in corn. The small bush he had so carefully planted to mark his cache was nowhere to be seen.

For several days the old man dug numerous holes throughout the corn patch in an attempt to locate his treasure, but it was all for naught. Dejected, he returned to California. Allen often spoke of making another journey to southwestern Tennessee to try to find his buried fortune, but before he had the chance, he passed away.

Since Allen's death in 1941, plows have cut into the soil on the old man's farm over many seasons. Eventually, the place was abandoned and it has since been overgrown with brush, trees, and briars. There is still talk of the fortune in silver coins buried somewhere out on the old Allen farm, but no one remembers precisely where the deceased farmer's three-acre truck patch was located.

Buried Kegs of
Gold and Silver Coins

Times were seldom easy for the early settlers of Coffee County, located near the southwestern end of the Cumberland Plateau. In most places the soil was far too thin to raise a decent crop, and the weather was either too hot or too cold, too wet or too dry. Only a few hardy souls lived in the relatively remote region, tough survivors who by and large shunned society, endured floods, droughts, Indian raids, and insect plagues, and planted their crops and raised their families.

As hard as it was to raise a crop in Coffee County, its residents were regularly subjected to even worse horrors during the War Between the States. Patrols of both the Union and Confederate armies moved through Coffee County, sometimes stopping at isolated farms and settlements and forcing the citizens to feed them. Livestock were often slaughtered and gardens were stripped of their produce. The residents, few and poorly armed, were powerless to stop the raids.

But even worse than the climate and the intrusion of the soldiers were the continuous attacks by outlaws. Toward the end of the Civil War, bands of renegade robbers and killers, sometimes composed of deserters from both armies, roamed much of central Tennessee and routinely ravaged the remote and defenseless settlements.

Cephus Wenten and his family had endured hardship for many years, but they had survived and, some might say, prospered. Cephus had no reason to believe they wouldn't be able to prevail against the gangs of outlaws as well.

Cephus was one of the few successful farmers in Coffee County and was well respected in the nearby town of Hillsboro. Because of the hard work and dedication of the entire Wenten family, Cephus always managed to produce a good crop and made fair money from it. Long distrustful of banks, Cephus stashed his earnings over the years in two old nail kegs which he kept buried in the yard near his house. No one knew for certain how much money the farmer had hidden, but reliable estimates place it at about 55,000 dollars in gold and silver coins.

One day in 1864, a group of men rode onto the Wenten farm and pulled guns on Cephus. The newcomers, a ragged band of outlaws known as the Brixie Gang, had been told of Wenten's hoard by companions in Hillsboro and had ridden out to the farm to steal it.

When Cephus Wenten refused to tell the gang members where he had hidden his money, they beat him severely with their pistols until his head was a bloody mass. Still, the farmer steadfastly refused to reveal the location of his savings. Presently, one of the outlaws tied a noose around Cephus's neck and threw the opposite end over a nearby oak tree. As three of the gang members hoisted the dazed and bleeding man up off the ground, Cephus kicked his legs violently and tore at the tightening noose to keep from choking. They watched the farmer struggle for a full minute, then let him drop to the ground. Holding a pistol to the farmer's head, the leader of the gang told him he one more chance to tell them where the money was hidden or he would hang for certain. Cephus still refused the outlaw's demands, and they pulled him up again and let him hang until the life was strangled out of him.

By this time, Mrs. Wenten was discovered hiding in the woods and was brought to the foot of the tree to gaze upon her dead husband, whose body was still swinging slightly. The outlaws told her she too would die if she did not tell them the location of the buried money. But Cephus Wenten had never confided to his wife the information sought by the gang, and a few moments later she lay dead at the foot of the tree, shot in the head.

During the next hour, three of the Wenten children were dragged from their hiding places. Each in turn was given the opportunity to reveal the location of the money but, like their mother, they were ignorant of the hiding place. All were killed.

For the rest of the day the outlaws dug at various locations around the Wenten farm but, finding no treasure, they finally left.

For sixty years Cephus Wenten's coin-filled nail kegs lay buried in the ground. After the family was murdered, people generally avoided the place and it fell into ruin. The neglected field grew over with brush and briars and the fences eventually rotted away.

Then one day in 1924, a local man accidentally discovered the treasure. Exploring around the abandoned Wenten farm, he spotted the edge of what apeared to be a small wooden barrel sticking up from the ground in the lot behind the sagging farmhouse. After removing some of the dirt from around it, he raised the heavy object to the surface and saw that it was an old nail keg. Breaking it open, his eyes grew big when he saw the small fortune in gold and silver coins that spilled onto the ground.

Believing he had accidentally stumbled onto someone's buried cache, the man looked around nervously for fear that he was being watched. Very carefully, he placed the coins in the keg, put the keg back in the hole, covered it up, and returned home.

The man never went back to the Wenten farm and told no one of his find until several years later, when he confided in his friend Peter Cunningham. Cunningham kept the secret of the buried coin cache for about a year and then decided to dig it up himself. Unfortunately, the day before he planned to travel to the old Wenten farm he had a stroke and died.

Many who reside in the foothills of the Cumberland Plateau are familiar with the tale of Cephus Wenten's buried coin cache. Several who would like to search for the treasure are intimidated by what they believe is a curse on the old farm.

They claim that the ghosts of Cephus Wenten and his family stand guard over the treasure.

VIRGINIA

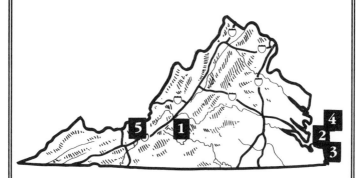

The Mysterious Beale Treasure

The best known and most sought-after lost treasure in the state of Virginia is the mysterious and elusive Beale cache. This buried fortune is said to consist of nearly 3,000 pounds of gold, 5,088 pounds of silver, and 13,000 dollars' worth of jewels. The Beale treasure has been the subject of books, magazine articles, and television programs, and one network news broadcast said the search for the Beale treasure was one of the longest and costliest in the history of the United States.

Specific directions to the fabulous Beale treasure can be found in three separate codes devised by Beale himself, as far as is known. Only one has ever been deciphered. The other two complex codes, though having been examined by cryptoanalysts and studied by computer and decoding experts, remain unbroken, and the location of the great treasure is as much a mystery today as it was when Thomas Jefferson Beale and eight friends buried it in Bedford County in 1819 and 1821.

Little is known of Beale's life. What is known is that early in 1817, he and twenty-nine other Virginians journeyed westward to New Mexico and Colorado. Two conflicting stories, neither proven, give Beale's reasons for leaving Virginia. One tale is that he shot his neighbor in Fincastle, Virginia, in a fight over a woman. Believing the man dead and fearing he would be hung for the deed, Beale fled west. The second tale, considerably less colorful, is that Beale gathered up friends for a buffalo-hunting and fur-trapping expedition to the western plains and mountains.

Whatever the reason, Beale and his companions eventually found themselves in south-central Colorado, searching for a pass into the higher reaches of the Rocky Mountains, where they planned to hunt beaver. As the party climbed the foothills of the great range, one of the men discovered a thick vein of gold in some exposed rock. Deciding that mining the ore would profit them more than trapping and selling furs, the men spent the next few years systematically excavating the precious metal from the rock matrix of the mountainside. They found silver nearby, and mined great quantities of it, too.

After eighteen months, they had an impressive stockpile of gold and silver. The men, all good friends, agreed to split the fortune evenly. They held a meeting and decided to send Beale and eight others back to Virginia to bury the rich hoard in a safe place. The others would keep working in the mines while awaiting the return of the Beale party.

On a bitterly cold afternoon in late November, Beale and his companions, along with two wagon loads of gold and silver nuggets, arrived at Goose Creek in Bedford County, Virginia. The party followed a narrow and seldom-used trail which paralleled the creek and led into a gap in the foothills of the Blue Ridge Mountains near Peaks of Otter. Once in the pass, Beale looked around until he found what he wanted—a place where he could bury the treasure. Snow began to fall, and the men worked swiftly, digging a square pit six feet deep. As the wind swirled the snow around them, the miners lined the floor and walls of this man-made vault with flat stones they found nearby. Into this chamber they placed the gold and silver from nearly two years' work in the Colorado mines. The nuggets were packed into iron cooking pots, the covers tightly secured with wire. The men filled the hole to the top with dirt and covered it with rocks and forest debris.

Beale and his party rested several days after the long journey from the west. They bought supplies and fresh riding stock, and started back in early December. They rejoined the other miners in the Colorado foothills nearly a month later.

Mining continued, and after almost two more years, another load of gold and silver was ready to be shipped east and buried with the previous cache. Beale was again chosen for the trip. The partners agreed to keep mining until they had enough gold and silver for a third and final trip to Virginia, where they would unearth the rich cache, divide it, and return to a normal life as wealthy men.

One morning in the third week of November in 1821, the wagons were loaded to capacity with the ore. Bidding farewell to those who remained to work in the mines, Beale and his companions began the second long journey back to the Blue Ridge Mountains.

Reaching the cache a little over a month later, Beale and his companions added the second load of gold and silver. When the hole refilled and camouflaged, Beale and his fellows decided to write a description of the secret location and its contents and leave it in the area for the others to find, should something happen to them. Over the next several days, Beale and a few of his partners devised a series of incredibly complex codes. They produced three sheets of paper, each covered with a series of numerals. These three papers have since been called the Beale Code, and have mystified researchers for well over a century.

Cipher Number One allegedly tells how to find the fabulous treasure and remains unbroken to this day. Cipher Number Two describes the complete contents of the treasure vault. Cipher Number Three supposedly lists the names of the thirty men who were to divide the treasure equally.

When the ciphers were completed, they were placed in a metal strongbox fastened with a stout lock. By agreement of the nine men who buried the ore, the locked box was given to one Robert Morris, a man they all knew and trusted. Morris, a quiet gentleman who ran a respectable inn at Lynchburg and often kept valuables for travelers, readily agreed to keep the strongbox for Beale and his friends.

At Morris's invitation, the miners stayed several days at the inn, resting. The day they left for Colorado, Beale told Morris that if someone did not return within ten years to claim the strongbox and its contents, he, Morris, was to open it. Beale also told Morris that within a few weeks he would mail him the information he would need to interpret the codes in the strongbox. Beale and his eight companions rode away from the inn a short time later, disappearing into the dense forest to the west. Morris never saw any of them again.

About two months later, Morris received a short letter from Beale that had been mailed from St. Louis. The letter reiterated what Beale had already told Morris—that the contents of the strongbox would be meaningless without the decoding keys. He said the necessary keys were in a sealed envelope with Morris's address on it. The envelope, according to Beale, was given to a friend in St. Louis with instructions to mail it to Morris in June, 1832. Morris never again heard from Beale, nor did he receive the envelope ten years later.

Although the designated time had elapsed, the trustworthy Morris refused to open the strongbox, thinking that someone from the Beale party would eventually return to claim it. Years passed and Morris soon forgot about the strongbox, which he had hidden away under some clutter in an old shed adjacent to the inn. One day, about twenty-three years after Beale had left the strongbox, Morris chanced upon it while searching the shed for a harness.

When Morris broke open the box, he first saw lying atop the contents a letter addressed to him. In elaborate detail, the letter told of the expedition to the west, the discovery of the gold and silver, and the subsequent trips to the Blue Ridge Mountains to bury the treasure. The letter ended by asking Morris to use the code to find and dig up the treasure. Morris was to divide it into thirty-one equal parts—one for each of the original participants and one for Morris himself.

Morris examined the three pieces of paper which bore the Beale Code. Each was written over with an apparently random series of numbers, ranging from single to quadruple digits. Intrigued, the innkeeper spent many hours trying to decipher the curious arrangements of numbers, but couldn't make any sense of them. For the next several years, Morris tried to decipher the complex Beale Code, but he eventually gave up.

Some time later, when Morris was convinced no one would return to claim the strongbox and its contents, he showed the codes and letters to a friend, James Ward. For months Ward pored over the three pieces of paper and eventually broke Cipher Number Two.

Purely by accident, Ward discovered this code was based on the Declaration of Independence. When finally deciphered, it read:

I have deposited in the county of Bedford about four miles from Buford's Inn in an excavation or vault six feet below the surface of the ground the following articles belonging to the parties whose names are given in number three herewith. The first deposit was ten hundred and fourteen pounds of gold and thirty-eight hundred pounds of silver. This was deposited November, 1819. The second deposit was made December, 1821, and consisted of nineteen hundred and seven pounds of gold and twelve hundred and eighty-eight pounds of silver. Also jewels obtained in St. Louis in exchange to save transportation and valued at thirteen thousand dollars. The above is packed securely in iron pots with iron covers. The vault is lined with stones and the vessels lie on solid rock and are covered with other stones. Paper number one describes the exact location of the vault so no difficulty will be had in finding it.

Ward, suspecting the other two codes would likewise be deciphered by using the Declaration of Independence, eagerly tackled them, but was soon disappointed to learn that they apparently had separate and independent keys. Ward was particularly interested in breaking Cipher Number One, which allegedly gave directions to the treasure site, but could make no sense of it whatsoever. *(The code, containing 520 numbers, is reproduced in its entirety at the end of the story.)*

Ward worked on the two unbroken codes for several months before giving up. With Morris's permission, Ward made the codes public.

Ever since the Beale Code was made known, hundreds of people—cryptographers, computer programmers, historians, treasure hunters, adventurers—have tried to decipher it. For many years, the Blue Ridge Mountains in and around Bedford County were fairly teeming with those who thought they had an inside track on the treasure. To date, however, the first and third codes remain unbroken, and the fabulous treasure is still hidden.

Although the Beale treasure is Virginia's best-known and most sought after, many believe it is nothing more than an elaborate hoax and that Thomas Jefferson Beale never existed! Skeptics have suggested that innkeeper Morris and his friend Ward fabricated the entire story. They point out that Thomas Jefferson, the third president of the United States and author of the Declaration of Independence, on which one code was based, had a penchant for writing in numerical codes and ciphers. It may also be worth noting that a man named Beale brought word to the east of the fantastic gold finds in California during the early 1800s.

If the Beale treasure is a hoax, two things remain to be explained. First of all, what would have been the purpose of such a trick? There appears no obvious or profitable motive for such a sophisticated and elaborate hoax. Both Morris and Ward shunned any kind of publicity, and neither profited from his association with the Beale treasure. Secondly, the sheer intricacy of the codes makes it seem unlikely to have been devised merely as a prank.

The Beale treasure probably does, in fact, exist and in exactly the amounts indicated by Beale himself in Cipher Two. Many who have researched the Beale story over the years have agreed on the authenticity of the events, the treasure, and the codes.

Beale Cipher Number One:

71, 194, 38, 1701, 89, 76, 11, 83, 1629, 48, 94, 63, 132, 16, 111, 95, 84, 341, 975, 14, 40, 64, 27, 81, 139, 213, 63, 90, 1120, 8, 15, 3, 126, 2018, 40, 74, 758, 485, 604, 230, 436, 664, 582, 150, 251, 284, 308, 231, 124, 211, 486, 225, 401, 370, 11, 101, 305, 139, 189, 17, 33, 88, 208, 193, 145, 1, 94, 73, 416, 918, 263, 28, 500, 538, 356, 117, 136, 219, 27, 176, 130, 10, 460, 25, 485, 18, 436, 65, 84, 200, 283, 118, 320, 138, 36, 416, 280, 15, 71, 224, 961, 44, 16, 401, 39, 88, 61, 304, 12, 21, 24, 283, 134, 92, 63, 246, 486, 682, 7, 219, 184, 360, 780, 18, 64, 463, 474, 131, 160, 79, 73, 440, 95, 18, 64, 581, 34, 69, 128, 367, 461, 17, 81, 12, 103, 820, 62, 116, 97, 103, 862, 70, 60, 1317, 471, 540, 208, 121, 890, 346, 36, 150, 59, 568, 614, 13, 120, 63, 219, 812, 2160, 1780, 99, 35, 18, 21, 136, 872, 15, 28, 170, 88, 4, 30, 44, 112, 18, 147, 436, 195, 320, 37, 122, 113, 6, 140, 8, 120,

305, 42, 58, 461, 44, 106, 301, 13, 408, 680, 93, 86, 116, 530, 82, 568, 9, 102, 38, 416, 89, 71, 216, 728, 965, 818, 2, 38, 121, 195, 14, 326, 148, 234, 18, 55, 131, 234, 361, 824, 5, 81, 623, 48, 961, 19, 26, 33, 10, 1101, 365, 92, 88, 181, 275, 346, 201, 206, 86, 36, 219, 320, 829, 840, 68, 326, 19, 48, 122, 65, 216, 284, 919, 861, 326, 985, 233, 64, 68, 232, 431, 960, 50, 29, 81, 216, 321, 603, 14, 612, 81, 360, 36, 51, 62, 194, 78, 60, 200, 314, 676, 112, 4, 28, 18, 61, 136, 247, 819, 921, 1060, 464, 895, 10, 6, 66, 119, 38, 41, 49, 612, 423, 962, 302, 294, 875, 78, 14, 23, 111, 109, 62, 31, 501, 823, 216, 280, 34, 24, 150, 1000, 162, 286, 19, 21, 17, 340, 19, 242, 31, 86, 234, 140, 607, 115, 33, 191, 67, 104, 86, 52, 88, 16, 80, 121, 67, 95, 122, 216, 548, 96, 11, 201, 77, 364, 218, 65, 667, 890, 236, 154, 211, 10, 98, 34, 119, 56, 216, 119, 71, 218, 1164, 1496, 1817, 51, 39, 210, 36, 3, 19, 540, 232, 22, 141, 617, 84, 290, 80, 46, 207, 411, 150, 29, 38, 46, 172, 85, 194, 36, 261, 543, 897, 624, 18, 212, 416, 127, 931, 19, 4, 63, 96, 12, 101, 418, 16, 140, 230, 460, 538, 19, 27, 88, 612, 1431, 90, 716, 275, 74, 83, 11, 426, 89, 72, 84, 1300, 1706, 814, 221, 132, 40, 102, 34, 858, 975, 1101, 84, 16, 79, 23, 16, 81, 122, 324, 403, 912, 227, 936, 447, 55, 86, 34, 43, 212, 107, 96, 314, 264, 1065, 323, 428, 601, 203, 124, 95, 216, 814, 2906, 654, 820, 2, 301, 112, 176, 213, 71, 87, 96, 202, 35, 10, 2, 41, 17, 84, 221, 736, 820, 214, 11, 60, 760.

Assateague Island Treasures

Like North Carolina, the state of Virginia has been associated with numerous tales of shipwrecks and lost treasures on or near its barrier islands. Among the more famous of Virginia's islands is Assateague, located just south of Maryland and adjacent to the uppermost Virginia portion of the Del-Mar-Va Peninsula.

Besides being a well-known location for hidden treasure, Assateague is famous for its population of wild horses, a small band of ponies slightly larger than Shetlands. Though the specific origin of these horses is unknown, it is believed by many researchers that they are descended from Spanish stock that came ashore following a shipwreck sometime in the 1700s.

An early treasure associated with Assateague Island is one that involves a ship carrying a fortune in gold. The year was 1852 and the ship was reportedly transporting a huge cargo of nuggets and ingots, all of which came from the rich California gold fields.

Following a relatively uneventful journey down the west coasts of North and South America, around Cape Horn, and northward up the western margin of the Atlantic Ocean, the vessel was struck by a violent storm just off the Virginia shore. Having difficulty maintaining control in the high winds and tossing sea, the captain attempted to steer the ship into Assateague Inlet; but the ship, its timbers already coming apart from the severe buffeting by wind and waves, struck bottom as it entered the shallow inlet.

Restrained by the shoal, it became a target for continuous pounding by the violent sea. Within an hour the vessel broke up, and masts, planks, and cargo were swept away to be deposited on nearby shores.

It has been reported that some of the gold was salvaged immediately following the disaster, but that the bulk of it disappeared into the soft, sandy bottom of the shoal where it remains today.

Charles Wilson was a successful seaman who captained many a merchant vessel up and down the Atlantic Coast. Heavy demand and generous compensation for his services made Wilson relatively well-to-do, but he soon discovered that fortunes were more easily obtained through piracy than by honest freighting.

Sometime in the 1740s Wilson abandoned the life of a well- respected sea captain and turned to raiding merchant vessels on the open sea. In no time at all, he accumulated millions of dollars' worth of gold and silver in the form of coins, ingots, and nuggets. It was widely rumored that Wilson buried portions of his wealth on Assateague Island.

In 1750, Wilson was finally captured by the British and transported in chains to England to be tried for his crimes. Found guilty of piracy and murder, he was sentenced to hang.

Two days before he was to ascend the gallows, Wilson penned a letter to his brother who lived in Charleston, South Carolina. The letter provided information on a treasure Wilson had buried on Assateague Island and even included a crude map of the area.

Oddly, this letter never reached Wilson's brother. Somehow it was misplaced and accidentally filed in the Office of British Naval Records, where it remained for almost 200 years! In 1948, the letter was accidentally discovered by a clerk.

In the letter, Wilson provided an inventory of the treasure he had buried on the island: "Ten ironbound chests, bars of silver, gold, diamonds, and jewels to the sum of 200,000 pounds sterling." Wilson meticulously described the location of the burial site as a point 100 paces north of the second inlet above Chincoteague Island. The chest was supposed to be buried three feet deep in a space bound by three cedar trees.

Unfortunately, the 200 years that had elapsed since the letter was written had seen numerous hurricanes and other severe storms sweep across Virginia's barrier islands, storms that altered coastlines, closed inlets, opened new ones, and uprooted and carried away many trees. Two-hundred-year-old maps of Assateague Island show a region quite different from what it looks like today.

Wilson's treasure was never found.

Charles Wilson is only one of many pirates reputed to have buried a fortune on Assateague Island. Sometime during the early 1800s, a pirate treasure was buried on the Atlantic side of the island near an old lighthouse. It did not stay buried long, however, for the act was witnessed by two young men who watched the pirates from a hiding place.

The two brothers, who lived on the peninsula, were returning from fishing at a favorite spot on Assateague Island. They had spent nearly an entire day casting their lines into the sea, but had little to show for their efforts. The sun was just beginning to set as they leisurely walked back toward their home.

Making their way along the dunes above the beach, the two men spotted a sailing ship dropping anchor some distance offshore. They paused to watch, and observed a rowboat being lowered into the water. A heavy object was then placed in the small craft, and within minutes the boat was filled with men who began rowing toward the shore.

Curious, the two fishermen hid in a nearby grove of trees and watched.

As it grew dark, the rowboat struck the beach and eight men climbed out. The brothers believed the newcomers had the look of pirates, and grew frightened.

Certain that they were alone on the beach, the leader of the pirates ordered the removal of a large wooden chest from the rowboat. It was obviously very heavy, for it took six of them to carry it. Leaving one man to watch the boat, the leader grabbed several shovels and, followed by the men carrying the chest, headed for another small grove of trees approximately one hundred yards north of where the two brothers lay in hiding.

About half an hour later, the seven pirates rejoined their companion at the boat. In a matter of just a few minutes, they replaced the shovels in the boat, climbed in, and began rowing back to the ship anchored several hundred yards offshore.

Suspecting the pirates had hidden some kind of treasure, the two brothers left their hiding place and followed the tracks of the sailors by the light of the half-moon, until they came to the place where the chest had been buried. Using only their hands, they laboriously removed the cover of sand and found the large wooden chest at a depth of three feet. Opening it, they discovered it was filled with gold and silver coins and jewelry. The excited brothers formulated plans to remove the chest and convert the contents to currency.

They left the chest where it was, hastily refilled the hole, and returned to their home. The next morning, they rented a large, durable cart along with an ox to pull it and returned to the beach. With great difficulty and using levers and heavy oak planks for ramps, the two men finally succeeded in loading the chest onto the ox cart. They covered it with a remnant of an old sail and drove to nearby Salisbury.

The brothers never revealed the exact contents of the trunk or its value, but they returned home the following day wealthy men. They built fine homes and never worked another day in their lives.

Treasure has been found more than once on Assateague Island. During the 1950s, a young sailor was hiking along a stretch of beach when he noticed a shiny red object in the sand. Picking it up, he was impressed with its brilliance and placed it in his pocket. During the course of his short stroll, he noticed several more of the red stones lying in the sand but passed them by, believing he had already found the prettiest one.

Several weeks later, the young man was visiting his mother in a nearby town and he gave her the stone as a present. Curious, the woman took it to a local jeweler who identified it as a ruby.

When this information was related to the son, he returned to the beach to look for more of the stones, but was unable to find any. He presumed the stone was from a long-forgotten cache buried in the area years earlier by pirates and subsequently uncovered by storm waves.

Assateague Island, like all of the barrier islands found along the east coast of North America, is composed of loosely consolidated sands. These sands are sometimes held together in isolated locations as a result of the clutching roots of trees and bushes. But more often than not, the loose sands are bare of vegetation and constantly shifted, rearranged, eroded, and deposited as a result of continuous winds and the ceaseless motion of the ocean waves. One day an area of beach may be stripped clean of its top layer of loose sand, exposing all manner of objects lying just below. The next day, the ocean currents may cover this same area with a fresh deposit of ocean sands carried in from the continental shelf.

The geography and character of Assateague Island continues to change in response to the elements, eternally confusing those who search for the long-lost treasures believed to reside there.

Sunken Gold
Near Virginia Beach

The year 1908 was known among Atlantic coast residents as the Year of the Storms. During that period dozens, perhaps hundreds, of ocean squalls and typhoons struck the east coast of North America causing incredible damage. Ocean-going vessels that plied Atlantic waters during this time also fell victim to the severe storms and one, the Dutch freighter *Edewijk,* was struck by a violent August hurricane and sank just offshore from Virginia Beach. When it went down, the *Edewijk* was carrying well over one million dollars' worth of pure Brazilian gold, a fortune that has never been recovered.

The country of Brazil has long been a magnet for foreign investors. The lure of fortunes to be made in timber, livestock, and minerals has attracted billions of dollars in investment money from American and European entrepreneurs.

For centuries, Brazil has attracted gold seekers in quantities that make the California gold rush of 1849 look tiny by comparison. Gold was first discovered in the gravelly bottom of a narrow stream by Portuguese explorers in 1570, and since then the mining of this precious ore, as well as of other metals, has been one of the mainstays of the country's economy. It is estimated that hundreds of millions of dollars in gold have been taken from Brazilian mines, with most of it being shipped overseas.

During the first decade of the 1900s, several successful European businessmen, many of whom already possessed important and lucrative mining interests, formed the Middle Atlantic Mining Consortium. This group, composed of citizens of France, England, Switzerland, and Belgium, was organized to finance the exploration for and the ultimate extraction of gold in the numerous granite outcrops northwest of Rio de Janeiro. The M.A.M.C. provided geologists, engineers, laborers, and a great deal of capital to open up dozens of extremely productive gold mines. Within months after operations began, huge profits were being reaped by the investors.

Because of some important political considerations as well as a desire to avoid paying what they considered to be excessive taxes, the M.A.M.C. wanted the gold shipped out of Brazil as soon as the ore was processed into bullion. Strong disagreements ensued among the members of the consortium, each insisting that their country was the best repository for the ore. Finally, after weeks of bickering, it was determined that the gold should be transported to and stored in a neutral country. The United States was eventually selected.

In August of 1908, the Dutch schooner *Edewijk* tied up in the Rio de Janeiro harbor. The four-masted vessel had been commissioned by the M.A.M.C. to transport over one million dollars' worth of pure gold to handlers in New York. The contracting of the *Edewijk,* a ship registered in the Netherlands, was another compromise reached by the members of the consortium.

Though the *Edewijk* was a converted ore-carrier and had seen years of service transporting heavy loads, it nearly foundered in the water under the great weight of the gold that was loaded into its hold. The captain of the ship expressed some concern at the displacement, but being accustomed to piloting a heavily laden ship, he assured the representatives of M.A.M.C. that the entire cargo would be delivered safely to the port of New York on or before the designated time.

The journey toward the United States was uneventful, and the *Edewijk* eventually reached the Florida coast. For two weeks, the captain of the ship had been repeatedly notified of growing storms in the Atlantic, but fortunately none were spotted near the route followed by the *Edewijk*.

As the vessel sailed northward along the Florida coast, however, a new storm began to form in the warm Atlantic waters about four hundred miles to the east. This embryonic hurricane was moving rapidly in a northwesterly direction toward the Carolina and Virginia coasts.

When the *Edewijk* reached a point near Cape Hatteras on the North Carolina coast, the storm, now a mature typhoon, was closing in. Squalls, which normally precede a major storm, struck the area, and the heavy-ballasted vessel was drenched. Maintaining the course was becoming difficult as visibility was reduced to only a few hundred feet. The ocean, relatively calm the previous day, was pitching and rolling in violent waves and creating major difficulties for the multi-masted schooner.

Because the *Edewijk*'s captain was determined to adhere to his schedule, he was not inclined to seek shelter from the storm among any of the shallow estuaries along the coast. Instead, he doggedly pursued the assigned route. He realized his mistake when, on passing False Cape near the North Carolina-Virginia border, the *Edewijk* began to take on water at a frightening rate.

After a quick review of his coastal charts, the captain decided to put in at Norfolk, some twenty-five miles away, and wait out the storm. He radioed the harbor and informed them of his impending arrival.

Fifteen minutes after the initial broadcast, the captain got on the radio again and informed the port authorities that the *Edewijk* was sinking and asked them to send help immediately. Moments later, radio transmission ceased altogether.

The violent storm raged for the next twenty-four hours, keeping area ships tied to the docks and effectively preventing any rescue attempt. When the hurricane finally let up during the late afternoon of the following day, several cutters hurried to the area where the *Edewijk* had sunk, but found only flotsam. There were no survivors.

When informed of the fate of the *Edewijk*, the members of the M.A.M.C. met and discussed the possibility of employing a team of salvagers to recover the gold from the hull of the sunken vessel. The businessmen voted against this option for two reasons. Such an operation would be costly, and the Brazilian mines were yielding so much gold at the time that the loss of the *Edewijk*'s cargo represented only a small fraction of their profits. In addition, the entrepreneurs knew they could collect the insurance on the loss of the *Edewijk*'s shipment.

To date no one has attempted to locate the treasure in the sunken *Edewijk*. Out on the ocean floor along the stretch of coastline between Norfolk, Virginia, and Cape Hatteras, North Carolina, dozens of wrecks lie on the shifting sandy bottom. Identifying which of these many sunken ships is the *Edewijk* would be difficult, but should the old four-masted sailing vessel ever be located, tons of gold lie waiting to be retrieved from the rotting hull.

Lafayette's Lost Shipment

On August 18, 1778, the Marquis de Lafayette and three of his compatriots watched helplessly from the shore of a small, remote Virginia island as the frigate *Dupré,* consumed by flames, sank beneath the shallow waters of the Atlantic. The French vessel was loaded with badly needed supplies and weapons intended for Lafayette's causes in the growing colonies. It was also transporting more than 50,000 dollars in gold bullion, a fortune that was carried to the bottom with a ship that has never been recovered.

Lafayette was born Marie Joseph Paul Yves Roch Gilbert du Motier in 1757. As a young man, Lafayette was strongly attracted to the liberal ideas of the Enlightenment. By the time he was twenty years of age he had served a stint in the French army and, after mustering out, he traveled to America to volunteer to fight for the colonies against British rule. Upon his arrival in Philadelphia in 1777, the Continental Congress awarded the young man the rank of major general.

Though France remained steadfastly neutral in the encounter between Great Britain and the colonists, Lafayette petitioned the French government time and again for funds, supplies, and weapons. Lafayette's calls for help stemmed from an unforgettable experience he had had shortly after arriving in the colonies: spending the winter with General George Washington and his troops at Valley Forge. The young Frenchman had been deeply moved by the dedication and patriotism of this half-starved, ragged, and barefoot army.

While the political leaders of France continued to ignore Lafayette's pleas for help, many of his agents succeeded in convincing several prominent French businessmen to donate money and supplies. All of this was handled clandestinely, as the French leaders were already extremely wary of showing any sympathy for the American colonists which might provoke British retaliation.

In July of 1778, several wealthy businessmen arranged for a secret shipment of weapons, ammunition, supplies, and more than 50,000 dollars in gold bullion to be delivered to the beleaguered colonists. The cargo was loaded onto the frigate *Dupré* at the northern French port of Le Havre, and the vessel immediately set sail for America via the Caribbean Sea.

The *Dupré* eventually arrived at the Virgin Islands in the Caribbean and from there proceeded toward the rendezvous point in Virginia. British ships regularly patrolled the waters in the area of the Bahama Islands, but the *Dupré* managed to reach the American coast near South Carolina undetected. The captain of the *Dupré* had orders to deliver the shipment to Lafayette and a company of his soldiers on remote and unpopulated Smith Island, located just east of the southern tip of what is known today as the Del-Mar-Va Peninsula. The *Dupré* kept cautiously close to the coast, cleverly evading numerous British blockades.

As the *Dupré* sailed across the mouth of Chesapeake Bay toward Smith Island, six small British warships, hidden among the tiny nearby islets, suddenly charged the French frigate. Dozens of cannons were aimed at the cargo-laden vessel, and when the attacking ships were within range, volley after volley was fired at the *Dupré*.

Nearly a full company of men led by Lafayette had assembled on Smith Island two days earlier, and now lay hidden in the wooded interior. When the firing began, the Frenchman, accompanied by three soldiers, ran to the beach, where they witnessed the sea battle in progress about a mile away.

Outnumbered and outgunned, the *Dupré* took several direct hits. The deck was blown apart, the masts and sails were destroyed, and a cannon ball opened up a hole in the hull at the water line. As fire raged out of control near the center deck, the crippled and broken *Dupré* slowly sank beneath the dark waves of the Atlantic. The sputtering and hissing sounds of flames meeting water were clearly audible to Lafayette.

After spending another two days in hiding on the island until they were certain the British ships had left the area, Lafayette and his company crossed Chesapeake Bay and returned, empty-handed, to the rest of the command.

Because the immediate concerns of the war demanded their full attention, Lafayette and his men gave little or no thought to the fortune in gold and supplies left lying on the sandy shelf between Smith Island and Cape Charles. The *Dupré* and her precious cargo eventually faded from the thoughts and memories of men caught up in the events of war and freedom.

Today, the decaying hulk of the *Dupré* rests approximately one hundred feet below the surface of the Atlantic, its naked ribs arcing upward from the sea floor. Amid the swirl of sand and the darting and bustling of numerous underwater life forms, hundreds of gold bars, spilled from the fractured hull of the French frigate, lie scattered about and all but forgotten.

At today's values, the 1778 shipment of French gold would be worth at least one million dollars.

John Crismo's Buried Coins

Early one autumn morning in 1887 on a remote ranch near Pecos, Texas, a young cowhand was trying to wake his bunkhouse companion, an elderly cowboy named John Crismo. When Crismo did not respond to his call, the boy walked over to his bunk and tried to shake him awake. The old man was dead.

The foreman was summoned, a burial was arranged, and as the owner of the ranch searched Crismo's belongings for the name of a relative, he chanced upon an old and well-worn diary. It held fascinating details of buried treasure, a treasure that may today be worth nearly four million dollars, and yet still lies buried beneath a few inches of soil and rock on a lonely mountainside in western Virginia.

The ranch owner pored over the often unintelligible handwriting in Crismo's diary and over several weeks pieced together the story of the buried fortune.

In 1846, when the United States declared war on Mexico, a very young John Crismo enlisted in the army in his home state of New York. Before leaving for foreign soil, Crismo got engaged to a local girl, and they agreed to marry when his enlistment was over. While Crismo was in Mexico, however, his betrothed fell ill, dying only days before he returned.

He never recovered from the loss of his sweetheart. He visited her grave, then mounted his horse and rode out of New York, never to return. For years, the young man roamed the wilderness of Pennsylvania and Ohio, keeping to himself and living like an Indian deep in the woods, craving neither the sight nor company of other humans.

When the War Between the States erupted, Crismo, wishing to return to combat, rode eastward into Pennsylvania, enlisted in the Union army, and was assigned to a cavalry regiment that was immediately ordered to Virginia.

Crismo's unit made several raids on farms and communities in western Virginia, taking livestock, food, and arms and often filling their own pockets with stolen money. In time, the cavalry force became little more than a gang of bandits robbing and looting its way across the Appalachian landscape.

One day, the unit was sent to patrol an area in southwestern Virginia, in Tazewell County. The men, about twenty-four in number, camped on the side of a mountain that overlooked a long narrow valley, flat and richly productive. At one end of the attractive valley was a mansion, and the prospect of finding something valuable at the fine home appealed to the raiding troops.

The valley and everything in it belonged to the eccentric James Grierson. Grierson, who had inherited a fortune, made another from cotton and livestock. The old bachelor owned thirty slaves and was thought the wealthiest man in western Virginia. He was reputed to be worth nearly a million dollars, a staggering amount at the time.

When the war broke out, Grierson, concerned about the safety of his fortune, withdrew all of his money from the area banks and converted it into gold coins. With the help of his favorite slave, Grierson packed the coins into canvas bags and buried them behind his barn.

Anticipating a successful raid, the cavalrymen rode into the valley and overran Grierson's farm, taking the owner prisoner and hanging him by his wrists from a tree limb in the yard. Throughout an intense and sometimes brutal interrogation, Grierson steadfastly refused to reveal where he'd buried his fortune, and the Union raiders soon realized that the old man preferred death to giving up his wealth. Grierson apparently did not survive his interrogation.

While Grierson was being tortured, Crismo befriended the old slave who knew where the plantation owner's fortune lay. With some cajoling and the promise of freedom, Crismo convinced the slave to show him where Grierson's wealth was buried. The slave took Crismo behind the barn, dug about two feet down, and pulled up one of the heavy sacks of gold coins. Crismo looked at it and told the slave not to tell any of the other cavalrymen about the treasure.

Several days later, the cavalry unit was assigned to another area several miles away. Once they had established camp and were awaiting further orders, Crismo returned to the Grierson farm under cover of night, and with the help of the old slave, dug up all the gold coins buried behind the barn. The two men loaded the gold onto a pair of horses and hauled it to where the cavalry had camped before raiding the Grierson plantation. A short distance from the old campground, Crismo and the black man dug a large hole, deposited the coins, and covered the cache with rocks and forest debris. Then they started for the new cavalry encampment. On the way, Crismo handed the old slave a fistful of gold coins he had taken from one of the sacks, and gave the man his freedom.

Crismo told none of his companions about the Grierson fortune when he returned. That night, by the dim light of the fire, Crismo sketched in his ragged diary a crude map showing about where the gold coins lay. In his rough and clumsy grammar, he added descriptions of the terrain and landmarks. The next day, the cavalry unit left Tazewell County for a new assignment in the eastern part of the state.

As the war went on, the regiment fought in several skirmishes, and in one, Crismo was seriously wounded. After a lengthy recovery in a field hospital, he was granted an honorable discharge and sent on his way. He first thought of returning to Tazewell County and digging up the gold, but continuing military action there would have made that difficult. So Crismo took his few belongings and traveled westward instead, roaming the country and regaining his health while biding his time until he could return to Virginia for the gold.

For many years, Crismo wandered the sparsely settled regions west of the Mississippi River, eventually finding his way to Texas. Traveling from town to town and taking odd jobs, the former Union cavalryman barely earned enough to survive. His few diary entries during this time suggest that the wound Crismo had suffered was giving him some serious problems and causing great pain. His writings also suggest that he was not mentally sound at that time.

Years passed, and Crismo eventually landed a job as a cowhand on a ranch near Pecos, Texas. Though much older than most cowboys and quite infirm, he proved a consistent and loyal worker up to the day he quietly passed away in his sleep.

In the years that followed, Crismo's diary passed through several hands and eventually wound up in the possession of a Pecos County man who decided to seek out the buried cache of coins. Using the clumsily-drawn, faded, and somewhat vague map, the searcher arrived at a small Virginia settlement called Aberdeen. Just north of the hamlet, the man located the long narrow valley that had once been part of the extensive Grierson plantation. The land was now state property, having reverted to government ownership when Grierson passed away leaving no heirs.

Just north of the old Grierson plantation was a prominent mountain, undoubtedly the one on which Crismo and his cavalry unit camped before attacking the farm. After exploring the mountain for several days, the searcher discovered what must have been the old campground. He found two Union army-issue canteens, numerous shell casings, and other items suggesting a temporary cavalry bivouac. While Crismo's directions were clear enough to this point, his diary entries never actually said on which side of the camp he buried the fortune. For weeks, the treasure hunter searched. He finally gave up and went back to Texas.

Crismo's diary was relegated to a high dusty shelf in a storeroom and in time was lost. The disappointed searcher never tried again to find the treasure.

Others have searched for John Crismo's buried coins. So-called experts, using metal detectors and dowsing rods, have combed the mountainside near the old cavalry camp, trying to find the four-million-dollar cache. No one knows what became of the diary, and the treasure remains hidden to this day.

Selected References

Anderson, Nina and Bill Anderson. *Southern Treasures*. Chester, Connecticut: The Globe Pequot Press, 1987.

Andrews, Ernest M. *Georgia's Fabulous Treasure Hoards*. Hapeville, Georgia: E.M. Andrews, 1966.

Arkansas Gazette. "Billion Dollar Golden Booty is Recovered." Little Rock, Arkansas: *Arkansas Gazette* (September 15, 1989).

Belcher, D.R. and Wade Chastain. "New Clues to the Carolinas' Incredible Spanish Treasure." *Treasure Search* (April, 1983).

Boren, Kerry Ross. "The Tortured Frenchman's Lost Tennessee Cache." *Lost Treasure* (November-December, 1984).

Brown, Dee. "Legends of the Confederate Gold." *Southern Magazine* (November, 1987).

Carson, Xanthus. "Col. Frisby's Lost Treasure." *True Treasure* (September-October, 1972).

_____. "Colonel Frisby's Lost Treasure." *Lost Treasure* (September, 1979).

Douglas, Hal. "Georgia Coin Cache." *Treasure* (June, 1987).

Duffy, Howard M. "Treasures of Stede Bonnet: The Bumbling Buccaneer." *Lost Treasure* (December, 1975).

_____. "Treasures of the Devil's Backbone." *Lost Treasure* (July, 1976).

_____. "Island Treasures Guarded by a Herd of Wild Horses." *Western Treasures* (December, 1976).

_____. "Hidden Hoard of the Pious Highwayman." *Lost Treasure* (June, 1977).

_____. "Find the Lost Fortune at Parlange Plantation." *Treasure Search* (August, 1977).

_____. "Missing Trove at the French Fort." *Lost Treasure* (January, 1979).

_____. "Clues to Chrétien Point's $625,000 Trove." *Treasure* (April, 1979).

_____. "Find the Lost Trove of Tensas Parish." *Treasure* (October, 1979).

_____. "Honey Island's Lost Trove." *Lost Treasure* (December, 1978).

_____. "Lead Plate Treasure." *Treasure Search* (December, 1988).

Ferguson, Jeff. "Treasure of the *York Castle*." *Lost Treasure* (August, 1978).

_____. "Virginia's Sunken French Gold." *Lost Treasure* (July, 1978).

_____. "Sunken Art Treasure." *Lost Treasure* (March, 1976).

_____. "Sunken Gold Off Virginia." *Lost Treasure* (December, 1975).

Harvey, Davis E. "Lost Alabama Silver." *Lost Treasure* (December, 1976).

Hein, Axel. "Alabama's Missing Spanish Gold." *Treasure Search* (August, 1988).

Henson, Michael Paul. "Lost Cherokee Mine in North Carolina." *Lost Treasure* (April, 1976).

_____. "Lost Silver Mine." *Lost Treasure* (January, 1979).

Howard, Duff. "Lost Plantation Treasure." *Lost Treasure* (December, 1978).

Howard, John. "Lost Tennessee Hoard." *Lost Treasure* (October, 1977).

Hughes, Dan. "Find Alabama's Ghost Town Treasure!" *Treasure Search* (October, 1977).

Jameson, W.C. *Buried Treasures of the Appalachians*. Little Rock, Arkansas: August House Publishers, Inc., 1991.

Kiedrowski, Leonard P. "Louisiana's Treasure Island." *True Treasure* (July-August, 1969).

Krippene, Ken. "New Clues to Blackbeard's South Carolina Buried Treasure." *Treasure* (January, 1978).

Kutac, C. "Fort de la Bulaye's Treasure." *True Treasure* (August, 1975).

_____. "Where to Hunt: Louisiana's $2,000,000 Plantation Treasure." *Treasure* (November, 1975).

Malach, Roman. "Bone Cave Gold." *Treasure Search* (June, 1985).

Masters, Al. "Multi-Million Dollar Treasure of Red Bone Cave." *Lost Treasure* (September, 1979).

McCarty, Jerry. *Louisiana-Mississippi Treasure Leads*. New Orleans, Louisiana: Treasure Publishers, 1966.

Mills, Robert C. "Hanged Man's Treasure." *Lost Treasure* (February, 1978).

_____. "Mississippi Train Robbery Cache." *Lost Treasure* (June, 1979).

_____. "Buried Silver Dollars." *Lost Treasure* (August, 1978).

_____. "Lost Yankee Gold." *Lost Treasure* (March, 1978).

Ruggles, Ray Duane. "Clues to Georgia's $100,000 Railroad Cache." *Treasure* (April, 1976).

Serpas, Paul F. *Tales of Louisiana Treasure*. Baton Rouge, Louisiana: Clater's Book Store, 1967.

Van Atchley, D. "Hidden Alabama Hoard." *Lost Treasure* (November, 1976).

Wade, Forest C. *Cry of the Eagle*. Cumming, Georgia: Wade Publishing, 1969.

Walker, Leroy. "Lost Silver Mine on Piney Creek." *Western Treasures* (February, 1976).

_____. "Leffew's Mysterious Mine." *Treasure* (October, 1981).

_____. "Lost Silver of the Cumberlands." *Treasure* (October, 1988).

Williams, Jerry. "Asa Smyth's Keg of Gold." *Treasure Search* (April, 1985).